THE SINISTER COURSE

~ A Sugarbury Falls Mystery ~

BY
DIANE WEINER

For information, email Cozy Cat Press at
cozycatpress@gmail.com
or visit our website at
www.cozycatpress.com

COZY CAT
PRESS

ISBN: 978-1-952579-19-6
Printed in the United States of America

10 9 8 7 6 5 4 3 2 1

This book is dedicated to our veterans, members of the military, and their families. Your sacrifices don't go unnoticed.

Chapter 1

~

Coralee's Outside Inn formed a silhouette against the surrounding Vermont mountains. The porch boards squeaked as Emily, Henry, and daughter Maddy walked past two elderly guests squabbling over a game of Scrabble, then into the lobby where they were greeted by the aroma of baked bread and the friendly smile of the owner.

Coralee smoothed her apron and fluffed her gray curls. "Emily, the books arrived this morning. I put a stack out on the table."

"I wonder if anyone will show up," said Emily. Even as she said it, she could see a dozen or so people already seated at tables. She pulled her hair into a loose knot at the back of her head and second guessed her choice of heavy linen slacks and a rayon top.

Coralee said, "I caught Amy practicing her autograph in between cleaning the rooms. She says she's a celebrity, being the subject of a best-selling novel and all."

Henry whispered into his wife's ear. "Do you think your sister's up to this?"

Emily looked at over at her younger sister who was short in stature, with a wide face that revealed her Down's Syndrome. Amy was already seated at a large table.

"After what she went through? I think she'll do fine."

Coralee said, "Come and meet my oldest and dearest friend." She led Henry and Emily through a maze of tables. "Ruth, here's our famous author and her husband, Henry. Emily, Ruth is a successful entrepreneur. She recently bought a summer home here."

Emily knew all about Ruth and guessed Coralee's thumbnail bio was for Henry's sake. "Welcome to Sugarbury Falls. I'm surprised we haven't seen you up here before."

"They don't call it the rat race for nothing. Seventy years old and never took more than a week's worth of vacation. That's about to change." Ruth held out her hand which sported a stack of diamond tennis bracelets and a cocktail ring the size of a ping pong ball. "I'm honored to meet you. I was greatly impacted by your story."

Coralee smoothed her apron. "Ruth, why don't you sit with Emily and her family?"

"That would be lovely. I'll need to save a spot for my assistant." She glared at her watch. "She should be here by now." She folded her arms and followed Emily to the table where she was introduced to Amy. "When Coralee told me your story, I decided to fund a private hospital for our overlooked veterans. I bought a few acres here in Sugarbury Falls."

"That's wonderful," said Emily. Henry nodded in agreement.

Ruth said, "Amy, dear, how have you been getting on now that you're back with your family? Thirty years is a long time to be gone."

Amy smiled. "I live with Mom and Drew, but it's not too far from here."

Emily interjected, "It's two hours by car, longer by train."

"I have a job this summer," said Amy. "I clean the rooms and help Coralee in the kitchen."

"Wonderful," said Ruth, with a tone typically reserved for a child. "Are you able to live by yourself?"

Emily jumped in. "Although Amy is very independent, she would need support to live on her own."

"Like from a facility?"

Emily explained. "Oh, no. She'd thrive in an indie-support home. There was one back in Westbrook where we used to live."

"Support? Like a doctor or nurse?"

"No, someone to make sure the groceries get bought and the bills get paid. Unfortunately, such homes are few and far between."

Feedback from a microphone pierced the air. Amy covered her ears. Coralee adjusted it, then introduced Emily and Amy to the gathered group.

Emily spoke about the thirty years of guilt she'd suffered believing Amy had drowned while under her watch and the miracle of finding her alive in the woods.

The audience had questions, mostly for Amy.

"Did Poppy hurt you?"

"No, never."

"Why didn't you try to escape?"

"Poppy said it wasn't safe to leave."

"Why did he take you in the first place?"

Emily took the mic. "He'd developed PTSD during the Vietnam War and was off his medication."

"Where is he now?"

"He died in prison," said Emily.

Coralee took the mic and invited the guests to the buffet table. Emily and Amy rose to get their plates.

"Wait!" Ruth stood up. "Coralee, I'd like to make an announcement, first."

"Of course."

Henry whispered, "What kind of an announcement?"

Emily shrugged her shoulders.

Ruth didn't need a mic. Her authoritative voice echoed throughout the room.

"My name is Ruth Winchester." Many of the guests nodded in recognition. "Yes, that Ruth Winchester. Anyway, I recently purchased several acres on the outskirts of town and planned on creating a small VA hospital, inspired by Emily's book. But after talking to Amy and her family, I've had a change of heart." She paused, and announced with the drama of an Academy Awards presenter, "I'm going to build an indie-support home."

A moment of silence preceded a crescendo of applause.

A man in the audience called out. "Support home? The last thing this town needs is a bunch of drug addicts and alcoholics living in our boundaries."

Another man stood up. "He's right. Those of us who aren't farmers, depend on our tourism industry. If word gets out…"

The first man continued, "You'll never get a permit passed. The citizens of this town won't allow it."

The enthusiasm bubbled from Ruth's mouth like newly popped champagne, ignoring the comments. "There's a barn on the property and land for farming. That's it! A food co-op run by the residents!"

"A hippy co-op run by druggies? That's all we need," said the second man.

A bearded man with wire-rimmed glasses stood up and threw his napkin on the table. "That was my land! You stole it out from under my nose."

The sound of a collective gasp echoed through the room. Ruth cleared her throat, keeping her poise. "Sir, that property was purchased fair and square at the foreclosure auction."

"I'm gonna sue, you know."

"You already tried. The court upheld the sale."

The audience's heads bobbed from side to side as if following a tennis match.

"I had the money. I was on the way to pay the money I owed." His face was the color of a sunburned Norwegian.

"That money was a day late and a dollar short," said Ruth. The veins in her neck throbbed beneath the thin fabric scarf she wore.

"You stole my family legacy. You aren't getting away with this." He kicked the chair, then grunted, knocking into a tray of desserts on his way out.

Coralee scooped up the mess and wiped off her hands. "There's more where that came from. Fresh cherry cobbler with French vanilla ice cream. Emily's books are for sale here at the table. Proceeds will be donated to the Vietnam Vets local chapter. And, of course, Emily and Amy will sign them for you."

Emily said, "Who was that rude man?"

Ruth answered, "His name is Buzz Gordon. What kind of a name is Buzz? He inherited the family farm and drove it into the ground, according to my realtor. Bank had been after him for a year to pay the back mortgage payments at the time of the auction." She looked around the room. "My assistant should've been here by now. Where in God's name is that girl?"

Henry said, "So you bought it fair and square. What's his problem?"

"He claims he'd come up with the money, but I beat him to it. The bank wasn't fair...blah, blah, blah. Between him and the couple who live next door to the property, I'm glad my own home is across town."

"The couple next door?" said Henry.

"I call them Mom and Pop. Dan and Nan White. Yes, you heard right. They didn't want the land to be purchased. Especially didn't want the traffic associated with living next to a hospital. My tires were slit when I went over with the keys the other day. I know it was them. I can imagine what they'll say when they hear it's going to be a halfway house."

Emily didn't like the term 'halfway house' and this time corrected Ruth. "It's an indie-support home."

An older woman with black curls and thick black glasses worked her way to the table.

"Finally. Luisa! Where were you? You missed dinner," said Ruth.

"Your lawyer called. He needed clarification on—she looked at the faces around the table—on a legal matter."

"Tonight? I hope you told him to call back in the morning."

"He said it was urgent. Confusion over..." Luisa paused. "Never mind. I took care of it. No worries."

She slid into the empty seat next to Ruth. "Looks like I made it in time for dessert."

"Luisa, what do you think of this? Instead of a VA hospital, I'm going to build a halfway house for people like Amy. And maybe get the farm working on the Gordon property. Start a co-op of sorts."

Luisa had to stop the cobbler from falling out of her open mouth. "You're not serious. We had this discussion."

"Dead serious."

"We already negotiated a deal. Are you sure you want to go in that direction?"

"Trusting my gut here. We'll talk more about it in the morning. I'll be right back. Have to powder my nose."

After Ruth left, Luisa said, "We spent months hashing out the details on a private VA hospital. Now she wants an indie support home? I'll have to contact her architect, the contractor, and the bank. Not to mention the publicity that's already gone out." She stood up. "I'd better get to work."

After the two women had left, Emily and Amy signed books for a while. When Ruth returned from the restroom, she chatted with Amy, asking for input on wall colors and furniture styles. Ruth committed to building a doghouse so Amy could bring her beagle, Snoopy. Of course, Amy thought the doghouse would go nicely next to the hypothetical fireplace in the middle of the living room. Ruth smiled and nodded.

Henry put his hand on Emily's shoulder. "I'll be right back." He left the dining room for the restroom in the lobby. On his way back to the dining room, a slender man wearing a black hoodie knocked into him. Henry hadn't noticed him at dinner and he didn't look as if he belonged. Who wears heavy jeans and a thick sweatshirt to a fancy event like this? He considered following him, but at that moment Emily and Maddy appeared in the lobby.

Henry said, "Where's Ruth?"

"Still talking to Amy."

Coralee came in from the porch where she'd been chatting with guests. "Are you heading home now?"

"Yes. It's been a long day. Amy's still lingering at the signing table. Can you make sure she doesn't stay up too late?"

"Of course. Isn't it wonderful, Ruth committing to funding the independent support home?"

"It certainly is. Did Ruth take a room here?"

"No. Luisa took a room, but Ruth's staying in her new cottage. I invited her back for Sunday brunch tomorrow morning. Why don't you all come over?"

Henry said, "Blueberry French Toast?"

Coralee nodded. "We'll see you in the morning."

Chapter 2

~

In the morning, Emily climbed down the loft ladder to get in a run before Henry and Maddy woke up. She cuddled her black cat, Chester, and dished out half a can of wet cat food. If she'd waited any longer, he'd have woken up Henry with his meowing. Even at this early hour, the heat and humidity stuck to her skin like melted glue the moment she stepped outside. The cabins in her community were arranged in a circle around Lake Pleasant. She spotted her neighbor, Kurt, walking his black lab. Prancer licked her hand.

Kurt said, "Mornings like these I wish I was back in Minnesota. How was the shindig at Coralee's last night?"

"You missed the drama. Coralee's wealthy friend announced she's going to build an indie-support home and start a co-op out at the old Gordon farm. The previous owner was there. Made a show about how she stole it at the foreclosure auction."

"It's about time Buzz Gordon got his butt thrown off the property. When his parents were alive, that place was thriving. Tourists always stopping to pick their own cherries and buy tomatoes. An indie-support home. Isn't that like one of those halfway houses?"

"Not exactly."

He let out a chuckle. "I'm sure Dan and Nan, the neighbors, are going to love that. Nasty people, those two. When old man Gordon was alive, they were constantly complaining about the tourist traffic or the trees hanging over into their property. You name it. Old man Gordon swore they vandalized his property on more than one occasion."

"Do they run a farm as well?"

"Don't really know what they do, but Dan bought himself one of them electric cars at Christmas. Those cars cost a bundle." Prancer tugged on the leash. "I better get going."

When she got home, she took a quick shower and knocked on Maddy's door and opened it a tad. "Are you coming to brunch with us?" Maddy put the pillow over her head. And groaned, "No, I'm tired."

"Teenagers," muttered Emily. She and Henry piled into his Jeep. The brunch line wrapped around the porch, but Coralee had reserved a table in the corner overlooking the golf course.

Coralee said, "Ruth should be here. She's never late."

Henry said, "Maybe the country life style is rubbing off on her. She did say she wanted to learn to relax." He pulled out Emily's chair and hugged Amy.

Emily said, "Did you have fun last night, Amy?"

"Yes. Only it was hard to get to sleep."

"All the excitement from our book signing?"

"No, the yelling from down the hall. People screaming, then I heard the door slam."

Luisa came into the dining room. "Has anyone seen Ruth? Her lawyer's been trying to reach her. She's not answering her phone. She was supposed to check in with me this morning. She's never late."

Coralee said, "She was supposed to be here almost an hour ago. This isn't like her. I'll drive out to her place if I can get things covered here."

Amy said, "I'll help you. I've helped you serve food before."

"Thanks, Amy dear."

Henry, disappointed at the lost prospect of French toast, took out his keys. "We'll drive. I've got the Jeep outside." Coralee directed them up a mountain road passing a one pump gas station and a Dairy Queen.

"She's really out of the way," said Emily.

"It's not too much further. There. Turn left. It's right around the bend." Henry pulled into the gravel driveway in front of a huge wooden cottage with large bay windows and solar panels. Coralee ran ahead and knocked on the door. "Ruth, are you there? It's Coralee."

Henry said, "Does she have a car?"

"Yes, a black BMW."

"I hate to point out the obvious, but I don't see a car. I don't see a garage."

"You're right. Where's the car?"

"You think she was in a crash? Henry, call the hospital."

Henry called the hospital; Emily rang the police station. They finished at the same time. Emily said, "No accidents were reported."

"And no one was brought into the hospital last night or this morning." Henry stuck his phone back in his pocket.

Coralee said, "She gave me a key so I could keep an eye on the place during the winter." She fumbled in her purse. "Here it is. I'm going in."

Emily said, "She probably went into town for groceries."

"That makes no sense. She knew she was coming to the inn for brunch and would've stopped afterwards, not before."

Henry took his phone back out of his pocket and called. "Amy, did Ruth show up at the inn?"

Amy said, "No, she's not here."

Henry said, "Can I talk to Luisa? Is she still there?" Luisa spoke through Henry's phone, "She hasn't shown up and didn't leave a message. She was supposed to handle an urgent matter but she…Never mind that now."

"Give us a call if you hear from her."

Coralee unlocked the front door and stepped onto a slate foyer. Sun streamed in through the ceiling skylight. "I'll check the kitchen. Emily, the master bedroom is upstairs."

"I'll check out back," said Henry.

Emily climbed the steps and entered the master bedroom The bed was neatly made with an Amish quilt. The nightlight in the socket by the bed was switched off. No clothes hanging on the chair like she'd have done had she gotten home late the night before.

Henry came up behind her, startling her.

"She's not here. I even checked the woods behind the house" He led the way down the stairs.

"Where could she be?" asked Coralee.

"Maybe she had a family emergency and headed back to the city."

"Her only living relative is a granddaughter. She's struggled on and off with addiction."

"So it's feasible she'd need help. We might as well head back."

As Henry drove back to the inn, Coralee and Emily kept their eyes peeled to each side of the road. By the time they got back to the inn, they were no closer to having an answer. Henry jumped out. "Did she park in this lot?"

Coralee said, "Where else would she have parked?"

"Let's comb through the lot and see if she dropped anything. I'll start on the far end." He didn't want to say what he was thinking. A rich, elderly woman was a prime target for an assault or even a kidnapping, but in Sugarbury Falls? He wondered if the granddaughter, wherever she was, had received a ransom note. He'd mention it to Megan and Ron.

Emily called out, "I found something!" Emily held up a crumpled piece of paper. "I bet this was meant for Ruth."

Henry said, "Where was it?"

"Right here in the last parking space."

"I saw a black BMW parked there when we arrived last night. It looked so sleek and sporty, I couldn't help notice."

Coralee said, "That's her car."

Emily said, "The note has an address and says to come immediately. Do you know where this is? I've never heard of this street."

Coralee looked over her shoulder. "It's not a street. It's the cemetery on the outskirts of town. Why on earth would someone ask to meet her there?"

Henry unlocked the Jeep. "Hop in. Call Megan."

Emily hated calling Megan on a Sunday morning. She and Pat were still newlyweds. She considered calling Megan's partner, Detective Ron Wooster, but knew he and Maddy's half-sister, Jessica, had spent the night in Burlington after attending a concert and weren't due back until later. She left messages for both.

Coralee called Ruth's New York City penthouse on the off chance her granddaughter was staying there or checking messages.

The farms stretched out further and further as they headed past the center of town. The road wound around a mountain and Emily looked for breaks in the guardrail as Henry crept along. They came down the other side, crossed over a covered bridge, and drove along a river.

Coralee cried out, "Look! By the water. Stop the car."

Henry pulled over. "Where?"

"The bench. By the lookout. It's on its side. Maybe Ruth veered off the road." She jumped out. "Look, the grass is trampled here."

Henry bent down and ran his hand over the grass. Then he examined the path leading to the river bank. "Tire tracks. Here in the dirt alongside the road."

Emily got a sick feeling in the pit of her stomach. "They lead right to the water."

Henry called 911. Coralee frantically searched the edge of the water. Emily followed the tire tracks until they disappeared into the water. She ran up behind Coralee, kicking over rocks on her way.

Coralee said, "I don't see any sign of her."

"The tire tracks lead to the water's edge."

"What if she...do you think?"

"Don't jump to conclusions. Even if the car went into the water, she'd have had time to get out and swim to shore. Cars take a while to go under. I've been in that situation before."

"Do you know what the locals call this stretch of road?"

"What?"

"Dead man's curve. And if she escaped from the car, why wouldn't she have contacted someone? She would have called me. And how would she have gotten back to the cottage without a car?"

Emily heard a siren scream towards them. In a blur, firetrucks, an ambulance, a police cruiser...

Megan must have gotten the message or the emergency call. She arrived at the scene in no time and checked out the evidence, taking a picture of the tire tracks. Later, she said, "I called for divers. We matched the tire tracks preliminarily to the type used on the model of the BMW Ruth was driving."

"That fast?" asked Henry.

"Technology. I sent the photo right to our data base."

Coralee said, "Maybe she got out. Let's check the area."

"I've got officers looking. Go home. This could take a while."

"I'm not leaving," said Coralee. "Not until I know what happened to my friend."

They sat in Henry's Jeep, waiting as the time passed like syrup from a tree tap. Divers had entered the water; a team was searching the area. Then they saw a diver emerge from the water and call out, "Over here. I've got something. There's a body inside."

Chapter 3

~

Emily sipped her third cup of coffee while Henry popped frozen French toast into the microwave.

"Poor Coralee." Emily's heart ached for her friend. "When do you think the police will have more information? How did Ruth wind up in the river?"

"Pat's doing the autopsy this morning. I'll drop by afterwards and see if he has any answers. She may have had a heart attack or seizure. He'll go over the medical history. The roads were dry and there was no sign of another car on the road. Megan didn't see skid marks."

"Coralee says she was healthy as a horse. She seemed to have wanted to get to the cemetery immediately after getting the note. I'll bet it was under the windshield of her car."

"I'm sure the car will be checked out. Could have been a mechanical problem." Henry knew it was unlikely, given the newness of the car and its stellar reputation. He put his mug in the sink. "I've got to get to the hospital. Don't you have to do that radio thing this morning?"

"It's called a podcast. Shouldn't take long. Afterwards, I'll go by the inn and see how Coralee's doing. I have to pick up the remaining books anyhow and I want to check in on Amy."

Henry gave her a kiss and went off to the hospital.

Emily finished breakfast, then got set for her podcast interview. She'd received the interview questions in advance and had jotted down her answers two days ago. She grabbed a glass of water, read over her notes, then connected to the podcast.

The interviewer asked, "How do you think your sister is adjusting to being home?"

"She's adjusted extremely well. She seems to have taken the whole ordeal in stride and is anxious to be on her own."

"Will you ever be able to forgive the man who abducted her?"

"He's no longer alive, and while I despised him for robbing our family of my sister for thirty years, I have begun to pity him. He was mentally ill with PTSD and unable to afford medical care. We as a society owe it to our veterans to provide affordable medical care."

"Are you still teaching now that you have a bestseller out there?"

"I enjoy teaching part-time at the college and plan to continue."

"Any idea what you'll be writing next?"

"Let's say the seed of an idea is beginning to take root."

After the podcast, Emily pulled on a pair of denim shorts and a striped polo shirt, then drove to the inn.

Coralee, sitting behind the front desk, was slumped over the computer as if too tired to hold herself up. Emily heard the hum of the vacuum in the dining room as she approached.

"Coralee?"

Coralee jumped. "You startled me. I was just getting the bills together for checkout. Monday's a busy day for checkouts."

"I'm so sorry about Ruth. You didn't sleep at all, did you?"

"No. I can't believe she's gone. Just like that. We've been friends since grade school, you know. I've got to try and contact her granddaughter. That's the only family she's got. I'm hoping Luisa has a number for her, or maybe I should go by the house. There's going to be food in her fridge that'll rot. I should toss it."

Emily knew it was common to focus on an aspect of control in such a situation. "Luisa must be rattled."

"She is. Poor dear didn't come down for breakfast. I sent Amy up with a tray and she said Luisa looked as though she'd been crying."

"I'll run by the house with you if you'd like."

"Thanks." She straightened up the papers on the desk. "I'll get Amy to keep an eye on the desk while we're gone."

Emily was proud Amy had demonstrated enough responsibility to be trusted with the task. "I'll drive."

The route to Ruth's house was in the opposite direction of the cemetery. Once they got through town, busy with summer tourists, the traffic was minimal. The gas station looked deserted, and the Dairy Queen hadn't yet opened for the day.

"Is Luisa going back today?"

"I think she's going to stick around to help make arrangements and tie up some loose ends. She's got to find another job now. Without a job, she can't afford to keep her apartment in the city."

"I imagine the granddaughter inherited everything. You said she's the only relative."

"I suppose, though I know Ruth didn't completely trust her. Ruth sent her to the best, most expensive drug rehab facilities and every time, she fell back on her habits. Poor Ruth was so stressed over it. Felt like she was failing her own dead daughter by not straightening the girl out."

"I suppose the will spells it out. Anyhow, I doubt anyone's going to throw Luisa out of her apartment right away." Emily pulled into the gravel driveway. The house looked different. Yesterday it was a friendly summer cottage promising relaxation. Today, it sat empty and held the last vestiges of Ruth's life. Emily shuddered.

Emily followed Coralee inside, flicking on the hall light even though the sun streaming through the skylight made it unnecessary.

"I'll start upstairs." Emily remembered the room next to the master bedroom sporting a desk and filing cabinet.

Coralee headed to the kitchen. "I'm going to clean out the fridge."

Upstairs, boxes of papers surrounded the filing cabinet. Emily rifled through and pulled out a file containing the deeds for both Ruth's city penthouse and her summer cottage. No mortgage info, just a copy of the checks Ruth had written for each.

When she and Henry had inherited his parents' cottage, it was already paid off. Making payments on their New York home had been stressful. Although they both had good salaries, they'd overstretched when buying what they considered their dream home. Little did they know how happy they'd be in a two-bedroom cabin shared with an adopted teenager, a three-legged dog, and a black cat.

Emily pulled out a second folder. She found a copy of Ruth's will right on top of the pile. It had been drawn up recently. *Had she had time to file it?* Underneath was an older will marked up with scribbles and margin notes.

She heard Coralee walking up the steps and walked partway down the stairs to meet her. "All done in the kitchen?"

"Yeah. She didn't have much in there. What did you find? Any contact info for her granddaughter?"

"Not yet. Looks like she changed her will recently. Come and take a look."

Coralee followed Emily back upstairs.

"The old will puts the estate in trust for Brianna, with contingencies that she stays drug and alcohol free. In this new version, looks like she's left everything to Brianna aside from some charity donations."

"Brianna was an excellent student and very level-headed up until her mother died. Then, things spiraled out of control. Ruth must have been convinced she'd gotten back on the right path."

Emily lifted out another file. "This has a list of what looks like hospitals—Pembroke Memorial, Memorial East, St. Bernadette's. She wrote notes. 'Veterans only, private, low cost' I remember she said something at dinner about how she was going to build a veteran's hospital on the Gordon property but changed her mind after talking to Amy."

Coralee looked over her shoulder. "Looks pretty detailed. Odd that she'd change her mind during a five-minute conversation with Amy. Ruth wasn't one to make hasty decisions."

"I have to admit I'm thrilled at the idea of an indie-support home, but you and I know for a fact there are veterans right here in town who aren't getting the care they need."

"Like Buck Howard with the amputated leg. He lives in a shack on the Gilbert property, poor man."

Emily nodded. "Henry sees him practically every week. He doesn't charge him, but the man needs specialized attention for those infections he keeps getting. Henry says given proper care, he'd be a candidate for a prosthesis."

"Ruth was a shark in the business world but had a heart of gold."

"Where might she have written Brianna's phone number or address?"

Coralee opened the mostly empty dresser drawers. "If they recovered her phone from the river, surely it won't work. She used to keep a date book in her purse. Again, her purse would be water logged if they were able to recover it." Rummaging through Ruth's things, Coralee found a small box with old calendars and address books. "We may be in luck." She flipped through the items. "Here. It's an older datebook, but I see Brianna right here under B." She stuck it in her purse. "I should get back to the inn. I'll try calling her from there."

"And if you want, I'll try getting in touch with her lawyer."

While Emily was with Coralee, Henry headed to the hospital and put in a few hours at the emergency department before heading down to the morgue. His best friend, Pat, was the medical examiner and had recently married Megan, one of the town's two homicide detectives.

Henry stepped out of the elevator and pulled open the door to Pat's office. "Did you finish with the autopsy already?"

"Yeah. There wasn't anyone ahead of her and Megan asked me to put a rush on it."

"Did you find evidence of a seizure or medical condition that may have caused the accident?" Henry poured himself a mug of coffee from Pat's machine and made a face. "Didn't we get you a nice espresso machine as a wedding present?"

"Like Megan would let me bring it to work? Not a chance." He picked up the report from his desk. "Toxicology showed she had a drink or two in her system, but not enough to cause impairment."

"And she was in good health, from what you saw?"

"Yeah. I spoke to her doctor and had her medical records sent."

"And?"

"Woman was heathy as a horse."

"So it's unlikely a seizure or heart attack was responsible for the accident." Henry paced the floor.

"Mechanical failure?" asked Pat. "Have they checked out the car?"

"Not yet. It's only been a day since they pulled it from the river. Just because you work fast, doesn't mean the police are as efficient."

"Don't let Megan hear you say that."

"Yeah, yeah. Want to grab lunch?"

"Chez cafeteria? You got it."

Chapter 4

~

On the way home from the hospital, Henry picked up Amy at the inn and brought her home for dinner. The aroma of stir fry filled the house and he found Maddy and Emily working in the kitchen. At the most random moments he was caught off guard by how happy he was with his family of three. He'd always felt complete when it was just the two of them, but when Maddy came into their lives…

Amy said, "Are you making Chinese food?"

"Something like that," said Emily. She and Maddy were vegetarian and while Maddy cubed the tofu, Emily stir fried peppers, onions, and baby corn. In a frying pan, she whisked chicken cubes around in sesame oil for Henry and Amy.

"How'd it go with Coralee?" asked Henry.

"She's understandably upset. We went by Ruth's house and found—not one—but two wills. The original left her estate in trust for her granddaughter, Brianna. Brianna had a drug addiction issue. The new version left everything except for a number of charitable donations to Brianna."

"An amended will. What prompted her to change it now?" Henry grabbed a beer from the fridge.

"Coralee thinks Ruth must have been convinced she'd beaten the addiction since she rewrote it without the restrictions."

"Didn't the assistant say something about contacting her lawyer at the book signing?"

"You're right, but looking through her files, she also had several real estate deals in the works. I found a list of hospitals and clinics Ruth was researching."

"Did Coralee contact the granddaughter?"

"She tried the number we found but didn't connect." Emily tossed a handful of vegetables into the pan. "Amy, can you set the table for us?"

"I wonder if she was ill," said Emily.

"Pat did the autopsy and went over her medical records. She was healthy as a horse. His words, not mine."

Amy opened the silverware drawer. "Ruth had a sore throat."

Emily had gotten used to Amy's out of the blue comments after being around her the past few months.

"I don't think she had a sore throat."

"Her voice sounded like her throat hurt."

"Last night? We talked to her at the table and I think her voice sounded fine."

"Not then. After."

"After the dinner? I think we all left around the same time."

Amy wasn't about to give up. She had her sister's stubborn streak in her. "Later, after you left. I was trying to go to sleep and I needed a glass of milk and a snack so I went to the kitchen and when I came up the steps, first the skinny man ran past me, then I saw Ruth. Her voice sounded funny."

"Are you sure it was her? It was late, right?"

"It was dark. She said 'Sleep tight' to me and her voice was scratchy like when Maddy files my nails. I asked if she wanted a sip of my milk and she said no."

Henry whispered to Emily when Amy carried the silverware into the dining room. "You know how she gets things mixed up. It was probably some other guest."

"Ruth wasn't staying at the inn. She had no reason to be upstairs. Besides, what was she doing there hours after the book signing?"

Maddy said, "Is it ready. Can we eat?"

They worked their way into the dining room. Maddy said, "Did they find out why Ruth was going to the cemetery? Or who left her the note?"

"No, not yet."

Maddy said, "I'll bet it was that guy who stood up and yelled at Ruth about buying the property and then stormed out."

Amy said, "Those men in the dining room were mad at her, right? They were all yelling." Amy was particularly sensitive to loud sounds. Emily attributed it to the years of relative silence she had living in the woods with Poppy.

Emily said, "The Gordon fellow left before anyone else and could have stuck the note on the windshield."

Henry said, "They can ask him for an alibi, but you know what he's going to say."

Emily nodded. She'd confronted the same alibi in researching every one of the true crime books she'd written. "He was at home, alone. Went straight there after he left the inn and stayed home the rest of the night watching TV. He does live alone, right?"

They'd just begun eating when Emily's phone rang. "Hi, Jessica. What's wrong? She's here. Sure. Come on over. We're about to eat dinner. Okay."

Henry said, "Something wrong?"

"It was Jessica. She said she has important news to tell Maddy. She and Ron are going to stop by after dinner."

Maddy said, "Do you think Ron proposed to her? They've been going out for over a year now. I'll bet she's going to ask me to be her maid of honor."

Emily said, "She wasn't giving off the vibe of someone who'd just been proposed to. She sounded worried. Guess we'll find out soon enough."

When they'd finished dinner, they cleared the table and moved into the living room. Henry put on a pot of coffee. They were watching *Jeopardy* when the bell rang.

Maddy got to the door first. Jessica, her half-sister, was in her late twenties and had Maddy's blonde hair and blue eyes. Ron Wooster, with his red hair and baby face, towered above Jessica—above all of them, really. Being gentle and soft spoken, his intimidating height gave him an air of authority and credibility. At least that's what his partner Megan said to his face. When he wasn't around, Megan affectionately referred to him as 'Opie' as in the old *Andy Griffith Show*.

Jessica and Ron sat on the sofa. Jessica hugged a throw pillow on her lap. Chester perched himself in his favorite sleeping place, on the back of the sofa behind her head.

"Can I get you coffee?" asked Henry.

"Not yet. Listen, Maddy and I might be in danger."

"What do you mean?" asked Emily.

Jessica said, "You've heard about that weird virus that's going around the Midwest, right? It's running rampant in the Chicago area. The prisons are releasing their non-violent criminals."

Maddy gasped. "Did our father get released?"

"Yes. That's what I came to tell you. Apparently using his own sperm to impregnate his infertility patients doesn't count as violent. I'm afraid he's going to try to make contact with us."

Henry said, "When Maddy ran away last year to meet him at the prison, he was disgusting the way he leered at her." He glanced at his daughter's expression and added, "Sorry, Maddy."

Maddy said, "What if he does come to Sugarbury Falls? I don't want anything to do with him."

Ron said, "We're keeping our eyes open. If he turns up, we'll put a watch on him. Let us know if anything happens out of the ordinary. Call me right away."

"I will."

Jessica said, "This is the last thing I needed to hear right now after finishing a stressful school year. I was all ready to lounge by the pool and give my brain a break. Now, I have to keep my guard up."

Ron swung his arm over her shoulder. "It's going to be all right. What would he gain by showing up in Sugarbury Falls? It's not like you and Maddy can offer him money and Henry says he not the paternal type."

Maddy said, "But Henry and Emily have money. What if he tried to kidnap me?"

Henry said, "Both you girls know the basics. Lock your doors, don't go out alone at night, stay hyper-vigilant. Not that I'll be letting Maddy out of the house without a chaperone." Maddy rolled her eyes. "You know I'm kidding. I trust you."

Emily said, "Ron, did you get word back on Ruth's car? Have the mechanics finished with it?"

"They're still working on it."

"Do you think it was the man who stood up and threatened her at the book signing? Buzz Gordon? He was angry she'd bought his farm at the foreclosure auction."

Henry added, "Two other gentlemen stood up and voiced their displeasure at having—and I quote—'drug addicts and alcoholics running around town.' They said it would hurt the tourism industry."

"It's an avenue we're looking into. Did you say something about coffee?"

Henry stood. "Coming right up."

Chapter 5

~

In the morning, Emily stopped by the inn and picked up Coralee after the breakfast crowd cleared. Coralee wanted to drive by the property Ruth had purchased to see if Buzz Gordon had moved back in, now that Ruth was gone.

"It's right there on the left," said Coralee.

"I don't see any cars here."

"I can't imagine he wouldn't have taken advantage of the situation. Come on."

They walked up to the farm house and tried the door. Locked. They circled around, peeking in the windows.

"Let's try the barn," said Coralee. "It's out back."

She led Emily to the barn and pulled open the unlocked door. Inside was smaller than it appeared from the outside. The damp earth smelled like manure though there were no horses or cows in sight. Emily and Coralee peeked into the stalls which were crowded with dry hay.

"Doesn't look like horses have been here in quite a while."

"Then what's with the smell?" said Coralee.

Emily shrugged. "I'll check the loft. If Buzz Gordon is hiding out here, it's a logical hiding place." She climbed the worn rungs, stopping to pull out a splinter. The damp, musty air made her sneeze. "No one's up here."

She backed down the ladder, and as she stepped off the last rung, a man's voice boomed. "Find what you were looking for?"

Emily's heart skipped a beat. Coralee came from around the bend and froze in her tracks. "Dan White. What are you doing in here?"

"I could ask the same. You're trespassing."

Coralee took a step forward and pointed a finger at him. "You are. This property belongs to a friend and there's no way she'd have minded me checking on it."

"Buzz gave me permission to look around. I hear the property's up for grabs again and this time I'm going to make sure I don't have to worry about neighbors."

"It's not Buzz's to sell. Why didn't you buy it in the first place? Oh, that's right. You couldn't afford it. Did you kill my friend for the chance to get your hands on it?"

"I didn't kill nobody. Not that I wanted to see a frickin' hospital pop up next door to my land, let alone a halfway house full of druggies."

"Where were you Saturday night?" asked Coralee.

"In my recliner watching TV. The Red Sox had a home game. Not that it's any of your business. Now, get off this property before I call the police on you."

"I could say the same."

"Old Buzz asked me to keep an eye on the place so go right ahead."

"Again, it isn't his property."

The barn door squeaked open. Nan White, a woman who looked to be in her mid-forties walked in. "What's going on here?"

Coralee said, "Your hubby says Buzz Gordon told him to keep an eye on the property, but it's no longer his property."

"The witch who bought it is dead now, so it's his."

"Doesn't work that way." Coralee looked her square in the eyes. "Ruth Winchester's estate owns it, not Buzz Gordon."

Emily put her hand on Coralee's shoulder. "Let's go."

"Out. Now!" shouted Dan. He grabbed a pitchfork that was leaning against the stall door. Emily pictured him with horns and a red cape.

Once they were back in the car, Emily said, "Let's ask the police to keep an eye on the property. Something's not right." She pulled out of the driveway.

Coralee said, "Wait a minute. Look, behind those trees. Isn't that a pick-up truck? Swing by."

Emily swung the wheel toward where the truck had parked but before she got to it, the driver peeled out of the space and zoomed down the road. "Did you get a good look at it?"

"Not really. It was old and red. I'll bet it belongs to Buzz Gordon."

"Let's stop at the police station on the way back."

The Sugarbury Falls police station was a brick building in the heart of downtown. With the tourists in town for the summer, parking was a bit of a challenge, but Emily found a spot down the street.

Inside, Ron Wooster was talking to an officer at the front desk. "Emily? Coralee? Everything okay? Jessica's father hasn't been in touch with Maddy, has he?"

Emily said, "No, nothing like that."

He waved them into his office. "Have a seat, both of you."

Emily said, "We want to report an incident over at the Gordon farm."

Coralee whispered, "It's technically no longer the Gordon farm. Ruth purchased it before she died."

"Anyhow, we ran into the neighbors, Dan and Nan White. They threatened us."

"And had no business being on the property," added Coralee.

"Threatened how?" asked the detective.

"Warned us to stay away. Threatened to call the police. Acted like they owned the land. As a matter of fact, they mentioned buying it now that it was up for grabs. Of course, unless Ruth's granddaughter decides to sell it, it's not for sale. She's the legal owner now."

"They've caused trouble before. When the bank sent an inspector over before the auction, Dan White pulled a shotgun on him. And someone set the storage shed on fire. We suspected Buzz Gordon at first, but turned out he had an alibi. A man walking his dog swore he saw Dan White over there with a can of gasoline the night of the fire."

"All to avoid having hospital traffic next door? Seems like overkill."

Coralee said, "Why didn't they outbid Ruth if they wanted it so badly?"

"They almost went into foreclosure themselves. Their own farm isn't doing well—at least it wasn't. They sold most of their animals and Dan tried one failed gimmick after another —a petting zoo, tractor rides—I'm surprised they mentioned buying the Gordon place. Then again, he did turn up in town with that new electric car. He got a windfall from somewhere, whether it was poker games, his own inheritance, or the lottery."

Ron's phone rang. "Excuse me a minute." He swiveled around to face the wall as if it would afford him privacy. "So the brakes were definitely cut? And it couldn't have happened due to the impact? Any other damage? Thanks." He swiveled back around.

Coralee said, "That was about my friend's car, right? Someone cut her brakes? So it wasn't an accident. She'd have been going downhill at that point and that's why she went into the river."

"I'm afraid it looks that way," said Ron.

Emily said, "Can't they get prints?"

"Not after the car was submerged in water."

Emily said, "There were a couple of old junkers behind the barn on the Gordon farm. Did Buzz know his way around cars? Or Dan White?"

Ron said, "That's the first thing I'm planning to check."

Coralee said, "I almost forgot about the red pickup truck. Emily spotted it hiding behind the trees when we were at the farm. Does Buzz Gordon own a red pickup truck?"

Ron clicked the keys on his computer. "He has a red pickup registered in his name."

"I knew it. He was spying on us. He took off as soon as Emily and I got back into the car."

"I'd suggest staying away from him and the Whites. Megan and I will take care of the investigating. You never know what people are capable of. And remember, if Maddy hears from her father, call me immediately."

"I will."

Chapter 6

~

Henry spent a busier than usual Tuesday morning in the ER, tending to a baby's ear infection, a sprained arm, heat stroke, and reassuring a young lady with a history of migraines that she didn't have a brain tumor.

He'd packed a Tupperware container of last night's leftovers for lunch. While he ate at his desk, he researched the Chicago health crisis responsible for letting Maddy's biological father out of prison. The mystery virus had already claimed hundreds of lives throughout the Chicago area and the medical community was at a loss for treating it. On top of that, the virus was spreading like wild fire throughout crowded institutions such as prisons and nursing homes.

Nothing regarding ankle monitoring, parole, or house arrest. How did they expect to keep tabs on the felons? He felt anger warming his face. He was not going to let Maddy's and Jessica's father near either of them. Should he decide to turn up in Sugarbury Falls, he'd be sorry. He drafted a letter to the prison board expressing his concern while he finished lunch. A fertility doctor who lies and uses his own sperm to impregnate his patients? It was assault. In what universe was assault considered non-violent?

He rinsed out the Tupperware container, then he called Maddy to make sure she hadn't heard from her—he could barely bring himself to use the word—father. Thankfully, she hadn't.

When he got back to the ER, the nurse pointed him toward a burn victim. The small hospital adequately met the majority of the town's needs, but it had its limits. It wasn't equipped to handle severe burns or trauma. Last summer he'd had to heli-vac a burn victim to Burlington. He breathed a sigh of relief as soon as he pulled the cubicle curtain open. The man, in his forties with a towel wrapped around his forearm, was conscious and wasn't screaming in pain.

"Hello, Doc."

"Good afternoon. What happened?"

The man opened the towel. "I was burning a mulch pile on my property and I guess the mulch had some fertilizer mixed in there. Flames burst up and this happened." He held up his arm. It was raw from his finger tips to his elbow.

"Ouch. We can give you something for the pain. Looks like the flames got the better of your chin, too. What about your torso or legs?"

"Naw. Just these spots. My wife said to run it under cold water. I hope that was the right thing to do."

"Yes, it was. I'm going to prescribe something for pain and a cream to keep it from getting infected. You're lucky. This could have been much worse."

"Thanks, Doc."

Henry grabbed his prescription pad and checked the name on the man's chart. Daniel White. A nurse whispered to him. "That's the second burn case we've had in the past few days."

"I don't remember anyone else coming in."

"It wasn't during your shift. Some guy came in with chemical burns to his eyes. Thank goodness he'd been wearing glasses or it could have been worse."

"Chemical burns from what?"

"Said something about working on his car and the steam burned his eyes. You'd have to ask Doc Thomas."

"He could have lost his sight that way. Idiot should have been wearing goggles."

"Fortunately, we rinsed it out good and the doc said there wouldn't be permanent damage."

"Next time he may not be as lucky. You gotta be careful. Always."

Things slowed down by late afternoon and Henry headed home. When he opened the door, he smelled garlic bread and realized how hungry he was. Spunky greeted him with a wagging tail.

Emily said, "How was your day?"

"Busy. Yours?"

"Also busy. Coralee and I went over to the property Ruth bought before she died. The neighbors showed up and threatened to call the police on us. We stopped by the police station to tell Ron. Oh, and a man in a red pickup truck was watching us from behind a tree. Ron looked up the license plate and it belongs to Buzz Gordon—you know—the man who stood up and threatened Ruth at the book signing."

"You have been busy."

"Oh, and I forgot the most important thing. Ron heard back from the police lab. The brakes on Ruth's car had been cut. She didn't stand a chance navigating that twisty downhill stretch without brakes. Her death wasn't an accident."

"Then, she was murdered. You don't cut someone's brakes if you don't mean to kill them. Has he got any suspects?"

"Not yet, but, of course, he should start with Buzz Gordon. I saw old junk cars on his property. If fixing up old cars is his hobby, he might know a thing or two about mechanics. And he left the signing early. Could have had plenty of time to cut Ruth's brakes and leave that note on the windshield asking to meet at the cemetery."

"Why did he need to leave the note if he knew the brakes were going to fail?"

"Coralee and I had the same thought and here's what we came up with. The route to Ruth's house is level and well lit. The path to the cemetery is dark, narrow, and is flanked by the river. Coralee says the stretch she was on when the brakes failed is known as dead man's curve. Maybe it was extra insurance that no one would save her and she couldn't ease over to the swale."

Maddy entered, her blond hair matted against her face. Emily smelled the sweat from across the room.

"Dad, when are you going to start teaching me how to drive? It's way too hot to ride a bike around in the summer."

"You just had your birthday, so let's make an appointment to get your learner's permit and I'll start teaching you on Mom's Audi."

Emily said, "Umm, I think she should learn on your Jeep, not my Audi."

Maddy had a quick retort. "How about you buy me my own car and you won't have to worry about it?" She paused but got no response from either of them. "Italian for dinner?"

Emily said, "Frozen garlic bread and spaghetti. Nothing fancy. How was your day?"

"Good. Two of the cats got adopted out of the cafe. A family with two daughters. I spent the afternoon helping set up a second cat tree, then hung out with Amy while she cleaned rooms. She's a perfectionist. Doesn't miss a single spot of dirt. And she sings while she cleans! She has a nice voice."

"She always had a gorgeous voice as well as an eye for details."

Henry said, "No contact from your father, right?"

"No. Do you think he's going to call me? Or show up?"

"I hope not, but it doesn't look like the prison put any restrictions on traveling and is sorely lacking in the accountability department. I wrote to the prison board expressing my displeasure. I read that there was a fatal shooting by one newly released prisoner hours after he left the jail. Non-violent criminals, my foot."

Emily said, "I can't believe they're letting felons out onto the streets."

"They claim it's unfair to cram the prisoners together. Inadequate supplies of soap for them to wash their hands. Really? Now public health officials are recommending masks, which the prisons can't afford to provide. All we need is a bunch of prisoners running through the streets wearing masks! What a load of bull. Those people were locked up for a reason and don't deserve to be out menacing society."

They sat down at the table and ate dinner. Maddy got up to get a second loaf of garlic bread out of the oven when her phone vibrated.

"Hello? Who's this?"

"Maddy. It's good to hear your voice. It's been a while." She screamed and cut off the call. Henry and Emily ran to her side.

Henry said, "Was that who I think it was? What did he say to you?"

"It was him. And he sounded like Jack Nicholson in that horror movie we watched together."

Emily grabbed her phone. "I'm calling Ron Wooster right now. He can warn Jessica."

Henry said, "Don't worry. If he shows up in town, I'm not letting him get within miles of you. You know I'll always protect you."

Emily punched the numbers into her phone. "Ron, it's Emily. He called Maddy. Just now. You have to do something. Can't they re-arrest him for harassment?"

"He called Jessica also. I can't do anything if I don't know where he is."

"Can't you trace the call?"

"Not as easy as it sounds, but I'll take care of it if it happens again. I'm sleeping on Jessica's sofa tonight."

"Thanks, Ron."

Henry said, "He can't do anything, right? I want to take out a restraining order in case he shows up here. I'll go by the station in the morning."

Chapter 7

~

Emily woke up early as usual and pulled on running shorts and a singlet. The air was so heavy she could barely breathe and her sinuses sensed rain. When she rounded the bend, she noticed lights on in the cabin Kurt had purchased for his daughter, Chloe. Chloe lived out of town and the small bungalow mostly sat empty with the exception of occasional seasonal renters. She jogged over to the cabin and in the driveway saw two vehicles—white delivery van and a red pick-up truck!

She squinted, trying to peer through the opening in the curtains. She jogged closer. It was definitely a man. She inched her way closer, then hugged the side of the cabin and carefully looked inside. It was him! A large man with a beard and glasses drinking a cup of coffee. Buzz Gordon. She scraped against the side of the cabin and the wood creaked. Her face flushed as she thought of the embarrassment she'd feel if she got caught. How would she explain herself? A lost earring? No way could she invent a plausible excuse in the blink of an eye and under pressure to boot.

She held her breath. Buzz peered through the curtains. Her heart pounded like a jackhammer. A hairy arm pressed against the glass. Now what? Was he as violent as he'd sounded the night of the book signing?

A hand snapped the curtains closed. She slunk to the ground and sighed with relief. When she was convinced he'd moved on, she pulled herself up and raced to the road looking for Kurt and Prancer. He'd be awake at this hour. Should she knock on his door, or continue in hopes of running into him? Her question answered itself. She heard Prancer bark as he led Kurt down the road. She ran over to them.

"Morning, Emily."

She reached over to pet Prancer who licked her hand. "Morning." She pointed toward the cabin. "I noticed lights on. Did you rent out Chloe's cabin?"

"Yeah. After the Gordon farm was put up for auction, Buzz came around asking if it was available."

"I thought you didn't like the man."

"I don't, but I can always use the rent money."

"Is he living alone?"

"Far as I know. Why?"

"There's that white van and a pickup truck. Are they both his?"

"The van's for work. He does some sort of delivery work. Guess the gig at the mechanic shop didn't work out."

"Mechanic shop?"

"Yeah. After the farm went downhill, I saw him working over at Bob's Auto when I bought some new tires."

"Then he's familiar with car mechanics."

"Judging by how quickly he left the auto shop and started the delivery job, I'm not sure how well he understands mechanics."

Someone cut Ruth Winchester's brake lines. That's what caused her to drive into the river. Buzz went off on her at Coralee's the night she was killed."

"So you're putting two and two together and think he had something to do with it?"

"Yeah. He had motive. And I saw him out at his old place spying on Coralee and me."

"Why were you and Coralee out there?"

"Coralee wanted to secure Ruth's property. Someone has to look it over—and good thing because those nosy neighbors came over. I wondered what business they had being there."

"I'm sure they'd love to buy it now that it's up for grabs again. Dan and Nan don't take kindly to neighbors."

"It's not up for grabs. Ruth may be dead, but she had plans for the property. No one's contacted Ruth's granddaughter or the attorney in charge of her estate yet."

Prancer tugged at his leash. Kurt shrugged his shoulders. "Good luck with that. Gotta go. Enjoy your run."

Emily fixated on the fact that Buzz at the least had rudimentary mechanical knowledge. And if he was burning through jobs, how did he have the money to pay Kurt's rent? After all, that's why she and Coralee suspected he was squatting out at his old farm. If he had a place to live, he had no business being parked out there like he was on a stakeout. Rain drops pinged against her head and she rushed home. Spunky barked at her the moment the door opened. She scratched his head. "Daddy will take you out later."

Henry said, "I'm not his daddy, for the hundredth time."

Emily smiled. "Just yanking your chain."

"Looks like you didn't escape the rain."

Emily kicked off her wet running shoes and laid them open against the front of the fridge to dry—a trick she'd learned decades ago from her high school cross country coach. "Not quite. I ran into Kurt. He's renting out Chloe's cabin. To Buzz Gordon. And Buzz not only has the pickup truck, he also has a company van. Kurt says he worked at Bob's Auto for a short time, which means he knows enough to cut someone's brake lines."

"He made a public threat at the book signing."

"The note I found was ripped from a small pad of paper. I wonder if there were any clues as to who owned it."

"Like an auto body shop logo? Can't be that easy. Besides, we'd have noticed a logo when we found it."

"He has a new job with a delivery company. I wonder what he's delivering."

"Does it matter?" asked Henry. "Unless someone spotted him following her that night."

"You mean witnesses? To him running Ruth's car off the road into the river?"

"Or to him tampering with the brakes."

"He's the only one who left early that night so who would've seen him?"

"There are other guests at the inn. Do you think the detectives questioned them all?"

"I don't know." He took a last swig of coffee and put the mug in the sink." I've got to get to the hospital. Are you working on your next book yet?"

"Still trying to settle on an idea."

"Maybe one of those Chicago prisoners will make for a good story. Felons running loose can only spell trouble. I swear if Maddy's so called 'father' shows up here and lays a finger on her, he's a dead man." He gave her a kiss. "See you later."

Emily tried writing after Henry left but the more she forced herself to think of an idea, the less likely the ideas seemed to appear. Writing the book about Amy's ordeal and doing the publicity work that came with it had drained her. She needed a week on a sunny island sipping pina coladas under a cabana right about now. Ruth's murder mystery simmered in the back of her head. Chapter one would be easy enough to write, but how would it end?

She showered and threw on a pair of cotton Bermuda shorts with a gauzy blouse and Birkenstock sandals, then headed over to Coralee's. When she arrived, Amy was sweeping the front porch. Her eyes lit up when she saw Emily.

"Em & Em! Are you here for breakfast?"

"No, honey. I already ate. I came to see Coralee."

"Did you eat French Toast?"

"Not on a weekday morning. I made oatmeal. Amy, did the detectives come by and talk to the guests?"

"Detective Megan was here yesterday. She asked me if I saw anything suspicious."

"And did you?"

"I was with you, remember?"

"Of course."

"But before you came, I saw something."

"What do you mean?"

"Right before you came for the book signing, Coralee asked me to check and see if there was enough parking, or if she had to let the guests park on the grass. I saw the bushes move and I thought it might be a stray cat so when I went closer, someone ran from behind the bushes and disappeared into the trees."

"Did you tell Detective Megan?"

"She didn't ask about before. She wanted to know about after we ate dinner."

"Can you describe who you saw?"

"He was wearing a hoodie tied under his chin and jeans with like a hole on the knee."

"You mean like a hole that was intentional? Like Maddy wears, or like they got ripped by accident?"

"Like Maddy wears."

"Was it a man or a woman? Tall or short? Fat or thin or medium size?"

"He was white and skinny. Not too tall; not too short."

"Did he have a beard or glasses?"

"No beard or glasses."

Emily trusted Amy's eye for details so she trusted the description. It couldn't have been Buzz Gordon she saw.

"Anything else?"

"He was wearing army boots, like Poppy used to wear. It's hot for army boots, right? Poppy used to say it was too hot to wear boots in the summer so he wore his tennis shoes instead."

"That's very helpful. Detective Megan may want to talk to you again. Is Coralee inside?"

"Yes. We just finished breakfast service."

While Amy resumed sweeping, Emily went inside and found Coralee.

"Coralee, Amy gave me a description of someone she saw the night Ruth was killed. Did you have a guest who wore a hoodie and army boots?"

"Army boots and a hoodie in this weather? No. I'm sure I'd have noticed."

"Did Megan talk to all the guests who were here that night?"

"Yes. The ones who were physically here. Saturday nights there's always entertainment in the gazebo at the park—and food trucks. I don't get the appeal of eating food off a dirty old truck." She made a face. "Not everyone stays in. But if they weren't here, they wouldn't have seen anything."

"Maybe they saw someone leaving or sneaking around before they left."

"One couple is already gone. They just came for the weekend."

"Anyone who's still here?"

"The older couple from Wisconsin. They went to the food trucks that night. I remember because the wife came and asked for Pepto-Bismol. See what I mean about eating from a truck? They went out to the porch to finish their coffee."

"Come on. Let's talk to them."

Coralee hung her apron on a hook and Emily followed her out to the porch where Amy had progressed to sweeping around back. She put on her inn keeper smile and walked over to the couple.

"Nice morning to be out. Not too hot yet as the sun is on the other side of the inn in the mornings. Are you enjoying your stay?"

The man in belted plaid shorts and a golf shirt said, "It's like a second honeymoon up here."

Emily said, "I heard you sampled the food trucks."

The wife said, "Boy, did he ever."

"I was doing fine until I tried the spicy barbeque sandwich."

Emily said, "While you were coming or going downtown Saturday night, did you see anyone who looked out of place, maybe lurking in the parking lot?"

The wife said, "Lurking in the parking lot? Wait. I recognize you from the flyer. You're the true crime author. No wonder you're asking about suspicious characters." She let out a small laugh and Emily smiled.

The man said to his wife, "Remember the phone call we overheard? When we came back, someone was wrapped in a poncho, sitting in the rocker right over there." He pointed toward the entrance, then turned to Emily. "It was late and quiet. I heard her say 'good job, that's why I love you' over the phone. She could have been talking to her kid back home is what I thought."

Emily said, "And you're sure it was a woman sitting here?"

"It was too dark to see. She was sitting in the shadows, but I know a woman's voice when I hear it."

"Could you tell if she was old or young? Anything unusual about her voice?"

"I don't know. Not an old or young voice. Normal. I wondered why she came out in the dark to talk and I figured she must live somewhere where it's earlier if she was talking to a kid. This was past midnight."

Emily said, "Maybe she didn't want to wake up whoever she was sharing the room with."

Coralee said, "Thanks for your help. If you want more coffee, the pot's still on even though the dining room is closed."

When they got inside, Luisa, Ruth's assistant, approached and spoke to Coralee. "I connected with Ruth's lawyer. She made you executrix of the will. We have to schedule a time for the two of you to get together."

"Me?" said Coralee, "Executrix of the will? What about Ruth's granddaughter?"

"They can't locate her," replied Luisa.

"Why doesn't the attorney handle the estate?"

"She must've trusted you. Do you want me to set up the appointment?"

"Yes. Here in Sugarbury Falls if possible. Other than her granddaughter, I don't know who to contact."

"I'll get a list from the lawyer and help you however I can," said Luisa. "I have nowhere to go seeing as I'm currently unemployed."

Chapter 8

~

When Henry got to the hospital, things were quiet so he sat down to check his emails. He opened one from a name he didn't recognize, assuming it was a patient with a question. He'd made it a habit to tell patients he could be reached through the hospital email, mostly to avoid a phone call.

"I'm coming for what's rightly mine. Tell Maddy to start packing."

Henry felt his stomach retch. He threw his stress ball across the room and grabbed the phone from his desk. He immediately called the police station.

Ron Wooster answered. "That son of a…No way he's getting near Maddy or Jessica."

"Can you call the prison in Chicago and have him re-arrested for harassment?"

"Honestly, we can't prove it's him making the calls or writing the emails."

"You've got to be kidding. You have to know…"

"Of course, I think it's him. I'm just saying we'll need more than that to arrest him."

"I'll email back and make it clear he'd better stay the heck out of Vermont."

"No. Ignore the email until we formulate a plan. The last thing we want to do is get him riled up so he comes storming into town after the girls."

Henry clenched his fists so hard he felt his own blood pressure skyrocketing. "Yeah, okay. If he comes anywhere near my daughter he's dead meat."

"Understood."

Henry slammed his phone onto his desk. Being a parent really had little if anything to do with biology. In the few short years Maddy had been with them, he felt like she'd been a part of him forever and nothing would stop him from protecting her. He called his friend Pat down in the morgue.

"Buddy, if you go off the deep end over this, you're going to get Maddy and Emily frightened. It's an email. Could have been sent from Siberia for all you know."

"But Maddy has to be careful."

"Of course, she does. Calm down before you scare her. And maybe she doesn't need to know about the email."

"Does Megan know anyone on the police force out in Chicago?"

"I don't know off hand. What would that do?"

"They could put a tail on the guy or something."

"I'm sure they can't do stuff like that on a whim. The old geezer is playing mind games if you ask me."

"You think so?"

"What's he want with Maddy or Jessica? It's not like either of them is rich and certainly he isn't having paternal feelings from what you've said in the past."

"Maybe you're right."

"It's a big game to him. I gotta go. They just brought in a body. So much for eating lunch. Hang in there, buddy. Try not to worry."

"I'll try."

Henry gathered himself together and went back to the floor. A patient with breathing issues was waiting.

"What's going on, ma'am? Trouble breathing?"

"Yeah. It's been on and off but I got scared today. Started wheezing bad."

"Do you have a history of asthma? Or allergies?"

"No, nothing of the kind."

"Open up and say *ah*." He shined the light at the back of her throat. "These look like burns. Did you eat something hot or breathe in any substances like bleach or cleaning products? That could be the cause of your sudden breathing issue."

"Um, no. Can't think of anything. Wait. I cleaned the bathroom with bleach yesterday."

"Then it would have given you trouble yesterday. Did you do any cleaning today? Polish silver or use stain remover?"

The woman laughed. "Silver? You're kidding, right?"

"How about pesticides or fertilizer?"

"Nope. Wait. I fed the roses."

He listened to her lungs and said, "And this is the first time you've had an attack like this?"

"First and hopefully last."

"I'll write you a prescription for an inhaler in case it happens again. The nurse will be in to show you how to use it. Meanwhile, pay attention to triggers. Plant food, grass insects...anything you think may set it off and we can go from there."

Thanks, doctor. You know, come to think of it, the crop duster was scheduled to fly over our farm this morning. You think it could be from that?"

"It's possible." Henry wrote out the prescription, noticing the name. Nan White. Dan and Nan. Mom and Pop. This was Dan White's wife. "Come back if your symptoms worsen."

His phone vibrated in his pocket. Pat was on the line.

"Miss me already?"

"I got a question for you."

"Shoot."

"The body that came in has corrosive chemical burns all over his hands and face."

"An explosion?"

"That's what I thought at first. Maybe he was cleaning his car engine and it exploded. Then I thought, the damage is more extensive than what I've seen in similar cases. I was wondering if I should report it to the police."

"You think foul play was involved?"

"I don't know. What if he was a terrorist making a bomb?"

"Why don't you ask your wife?"

"I tried, but she's out on another case at the moment and I need to sign off on this body…or not."

"Who brought him in?"

"That's another thing. No one saw him come in. A nurse found him dead in a waiting room seat. I can't imagine he was able to drive himself over."

"An accomplice, perhaps? I'd definitely call the station."

"Okay, buddy. I'll try Megan one more time but if she isn't available, I'll make the call. Back to work. Thanks."

Henry went back to the floor and recognized Buck Howard, a Vietnam vet and frequent flier due to his diabetes and high blood pressure. He often ran out of money to buy his meds and either cut down his doses or skipped them all together.

A vet hospital here in town would have been helpful. Not that an indie-support house that would benefit people like Amy wasn't important, but this was a matter of life and death. He'd never say that to Emily knowing how much she loved Amy. Too bad Ruth Winchester didn't leave provisions for both.

Buck's clothes were dirty and he smelled of old food and cigarette smoke. He'd lost weight since the last time he'd been in. "What's going on, Buck?" Henry snapped on a pair of latex gloves.

"It's this sore on my foot. I think it's infected or something."

"You been getting enough to eat these days?" Buck shrugged his shoulders. Henry examined his foot. "It's infected all right. This must have been brewing for a while. I told you to come in as soon as something like this happened."

"You know I can't pay for these visits and I feel like a heel taking charity."

"It's not charity. You gave years of your life serving in the army to protect our country. You deserve medical care." Henry wondered how long it would be before Buck lost that foot.

"I'm still trying to find a job you know"

"I remember. How about tutoring kids that had trouble during the school year? You've got a college degree."

"Look at me. Parents would be scared to have me sitting one on one with their kid. I was helping out at the local farms and doing light construction work but now I can barely walk."

"You worked out at the Gordon farm, didn't you?"

"Yeah. Back when the old man was alive. When he died, I built a second barn for his incompetent son and didn't get paid a dime."

"A second barn? Why did he need a second barn if the farm was falling apart?"

"Beats me. And it was way out at the edge of his property. You don't want your animals so close to a neighbor's property line if you ask me. There was no room for a horse run and with the trees surrounding it, he'd have to move the cows in order for them to graze. Obviously he didn't have too many smarts or he'd have made a go of the place."

Henry cleaned and wrapped the wound himself and wouldn't charge Buck for the visit. "Look, you've got to keep on top of this wound. Clean it and take your antibiotics. And you have to stay on top of your blood sugar. Super careful with the diet and I want to see you back in a few days."

"Got it, Doc. Thank you."

After he left, Henry had a few minutes to catch his breath. In an ER which most often saw nothing more serious than broken bones and bee stings, he'd seen the patient with burns —Dan White. Then, there was a man down in the morgue who'd died of corrosive burns. And Nan White with no history of asthma, with breathing difficulties and burns in her throat. Dan White. Nan White.

He clicked a few keys and checked their addresses. Sure enough, they resided at the same address. And they'd listed each other as emergency contacts. Whatever caused the burns affected both of them so it most likely came from their home. What about the man in the morgue? Was he affected by the same source? If there were a source causing this type of damage, it could become a public health issue. He picked up the phone.

"Hey, Pat. I've got a question for you. Do you have an ID on the dead guy with the burns?"

"Yeah. Just a second. Okay, his name is Ransom Harris."

"Does he have an address or a place of employment?"

"Not like he had time to fill out a patient intake form. They found a wallet with a driver's license, that's it. What is this, buddy? You know the guy?"

"No, but I think whatever caused his burns may be related to issues with two patients I saw in the ER. One had chemical burns on his arms and face; his wife was in just now with breathing issues but I noticed burns in the back of her throat like she breathed in something corrosive. And this guy's death must have been thought suspicious enough to warrant an autopsy."

"Suspicious because of how he was dumped here. Whoever left him may be responsible for the death. Hang on, I'll get the address."

While Henry waited, he pieced together the timeline. His death and Nan White's problems could stem from the same occurrence.

Pat said, "Okay, so Mr. Harris lived out by the cemetery on the outskirts of town. As far as employment, I have no idea. I'm sure Megan will know after they get a chance to investigate."

"And time of death?"

"He came into the emergency room a little after noon."

"Thanks. I'll check and see how close it is to the White's place."

"Let me know if Megan finds out where he worked and if you come up with any clues as to what caused the burns. I'm afraid it may have to do with pesticide spraying. I had a case last summer where a patient was too close when the spraying occurred. I saw in the paper they were planning on sending planes out this week. The mosquitos are wicked this year."

"I gotcha."

Henry looked at Nan and Dan's address. It was across town from Ransom Harris's address. That didn't mean their place of employment wasn't closer, or that they happened to be in the same place when the spraying occurred. He checked the intake records for the hospital. No one else had been admitted this morning with similar problems. Then he went online to check the newspaper article he'd seen about the spraying. He scrolled through the time table. It was possible. If there was a flaw in the spraying, more lives could be in danger. He put in a call to town hall.

Chapter 9

~

When Henry opened the front door, Spunky was waiting, tail wagging. Henry scratched him behind his ears, made sure no one was watching, and gave him a kiss on top of his nose.

Maddy came in from the kitchen eating a container of yogurt. "Can you take me driving today?"

"Driving, huh. I guess. Hmm."

"What? I have my permit now."

"It's just…I haven't had a chance to update my will."

Maddy rolled her eyes at him. "You don't need to tell me anything. I've been studying YouTube videos. Driving looks like a piece of cake."

"Whatever you say. Let me change out of these clothes and grab a snack first. Where's Emily?"

"She went over to the inn to talk to Coralee about something."

"Did you take Spunky for a walk this afternoon?"

"Yep. Kurt was out with Prancer. Poor Spunky. Spunky tried to play and Prancer acts like a grumpy old man."

"Text Emily and tell her we're going driving. I'll be ready in a few minutes."

Henry liked feeling in control and teaching Maddy how to drive would be the antithesis. He'd give her clear directions and break it down into manageable steps. How hard could it be? Everyone he knew who was old enough to drive had a license, right?

"I'm ready," said Maddy.

He wasn't as certain. "Let's go."

"Give me the keys. You still need the key, right? Jessica's car starts by pushing a button."

"You still need to have a key nearby." He watched her struggle to get the key in properly. "The peddle on the right is the gas, also known as the accelerator. The one in the middle is the brake. When you slow down, you have to push it down gradually."

"Brake on the right, pedal in the middle. Press down hard to make the car stop. Got it."

"Ha ha. You're a regular Jay Leno."

"Jay who?"

"Never mind."

After watching her roll her eyes while he spoke about finding the proper seat position and adjusting mirrors, he knew this was going to require patience.

"Okay, put the Jeep in reverse. It's the *R*. Maybe I should get it out of the driveway for you."

"I got this."

"Check your rearview mirror. Make sure no one's walking past before you pull out."

"Okay. There's a kid on a bike. He can get out of the way, right?"

"You're impossible." She wasn't exactly smooth about it, but Maddy managed to get the Jeep out of the driveway and onto the road. "Speed limit's 30."

"I'm going like 20."

Now Henry was the one rolling his eyes. "Let's go away from town, it's getting to be rush hour."

"Rush hour? We had rush hour when I lived in Chicago. Sugarbury Falls doesn't have rush hour."

The Whites lived right next door to the Gordon farm which Ruth Winchester had purchased. Henry wondered if there were other neighbors who might be at risk from the pesticide spraying. "Turn right. No, you have to slow down into the turn!"

"You're making me nervous. Stop." She slammed on the brake.

"What are you doing? If you crash the Jeep our insurance will skyrocket." He took a deep breath. "Okay. I'll be quiet. Keep going straight."

She was better at this than he expected her to be. As they progressed, she handled the Jeep fairly smoothly. He knew it would've been easier for her to start learning on a smaller vehicle, but no way would Emily allow him to teach her in the Audi. They arrived at the Gordon—no, the Winchester—property.

"Where do I go?"

"Pull onto the side road and we'll go around to the back of the farm. I'm curious about something."

They drove behind the property. Henry said, "Slow down."

"I'm doing 15 mph."

"I'm looking for something. One of my patients said there was a second barn out here."

"Is that it?"

Henry squinted out the window. "It must be. Stop. Put your foot slowly on the brake, and..." The car lunged forward, then stopped. Henry counted to ten. "Okay, I just want to have a peek. You can wait here if you want to."

"No, I'll come." She followed him behind the trees which mostly obscured the view from the road. "It looks like there was a fire."

One side of the wooden barn looked like an overly roasted marshmallow. Part of the wall was charred. "Sure does. It still smells, like it was recent."

"It smells like rotten eggs," said Maddy. "Do you think the hens were sitting on eggs and then..."

"No. It smells like sulphur."

Henry walked around to the other side of the barn, while Maddy headed toward the White's property.

When he came upon the barn doors, he saw tire tracks. He snapped a picture with his phone, then went out to the access road. A crumpled fast food wrapper and plastic cup littered the grass.

He walked back and checked out the grassy area in front of the barn. Something shiny caught his eye. He bent down and picked up a tire rim. Not far from that spot, he saw an old car battery. The mystery of the sulphur odor—solved. Maddy ran toward him.

"What's that?"

He was still holding the rim. "Maybe they've got a chop shop going on here. What's in your hand?"

She held up a travel coffee mug. "It has the initials NW. And there's lipstick on the rim."

"NW is most likely Nan White."

Maddy pointed. "Whose house is that?"

"That's where Dan and Nan White live. Why are they going back and forth to this property? And I wonder if Buzz Gordon knew they were crossing property lines."

Maddy said, "Shush. What's that?"

"What?"

"Do you hear the rustling?"

Henry remained still. "No, I don't hear anything."

She pointed to a tree. "The branch…it's moving."

"It's probably an animal."

"Now do you hear something?"

Henry did. It sounded like human grunting. "Go back to the Jeep and lock the doors." He ran into the woods, looking in both directions, listening for footsteps. If someone had been out there, he'd lost them. Maddy caught up to him. "Did you see anyone?"

"No. Too late. Maybe it was an animal. I told you to stay in the Jeep."

Ignoring him, Maddy pointed to the ground. "Do animals leave footprints? They look about the size of your feet so it must be a man who was out here. These look fresh."

Henry bent down, then followed them for a short while until the overgrown grass obscured them. Then he heard an engine start.

"They're getting away," said Maddy.

"Whoever it was is gone now. By the way, never rev the engine like that."

"Who do you think it was? The neighbor?"

"Or the man who used to own the place. Maybe he came out to work on the junk cars."

"Or…"

"What, Maddy?"

"What if it was my father? What if he followed me here to Sugarbury Falls?"

"There's no reason to jump to conclusions. It's more likely it was the neighbor or Buzz Gordon."

"Maybe I should call Jessica."

"Let's get out of here. Do you want me to drive home?"

"Not a chance. I'm getting the hang of this."

When they got back to the house, Henry exhaled. First driving lesson done and they'd made it back alive. In spite of the intruder. The thought of Maddy's 'father' being in town stirred a hornet's nest of anger. Shaking it off, he wondered how long it would take before Maddy was ready to go for her license. What if she'd been driving by herself and her 'father' found her? Suppose he hadn't been with her out at the Gordon property? Maddy had taken the required driver's education course this past spring and judging by today's lesson, it wouldn't take long. First things first.

Spunky waited in the window, nose parting the curtains, tail wagging. Chester slept perched on the back of the sofa.

Emily said, "How did driving go?"

Maddy responded, "Great. I should be ready in a few weeks to take the test."

Henry cleared his throat. "Don't you have to turn sixteen first?"

"Hypothetically I'd be ready. What's for dinner?"

Emily said, "I made veggie burgers and sweet potato fries for all of us."

Henry had gotten used to frequent vegetarian meals at home, though once in a while he craved a good steak. "How's Coralee doing?" He grabbed three plates from the cabinet.

"She's sad, of course, about losing Ruth. Tomorrow she meets with the attorney about Ruth's estate. She can't locate

Ruth's granddaughter. Hopefully, the lawyer has more up to date information."

Henry said, "I wonder how the police are coming along on leads. Maddy and I drove out to the Gordon farm to practice her driving. Looks like there'd been a recent fire. Buzz Gordon had old car parts lying around. Shouldn't he have cleared out when Ruth bought the property?"

"I didn't see any car parts lying around."

"I'm talking about the second barn. The one way back that abuts the White's farm."

"How did you find a second barn?"

"One of my patients mentioned it and I figured that area was a good spot to take Maddy driving since it's so remote." He grabbed silverware from the drawer while Maddy put out glasses and retrieved the iced tea from the fridge.

Maddy said, "Henry saw tire marks and I found a travel mug with the initials NW. Henry thinks that's Nan White."

"On the Gordon property?" asked Emily.

"Yep."

Henry said, "Nan White came into the ER with breathing problems today and I recently saw Dan White with chemical burns on his arms and face. I called town hall but had to leave a message. I think they may have been spraying in that area and perhaps released too much pesticide. Also, Pat got a body down in the morgue with chemical burns bad enough to kill him."

"From pesticides? Really?" Emily put the veggie burgers on a plate and grabbed the buns.

"Maddy found Nan White's mug on the Gordon property, and someone had driven from the access road to the barn. I wonder what's hiding in the barn."

"What do you have in mind?"

"I don't know. It was probably pesticides causing the trouble."

Emily put the serving plate on the table. "Have you seen the news today? There was an explosion out in the town hall parking lot following a budget meeting."

"Did anyone get hurt?"

"Someone died, but they won't release his name until they notify next of kin."

"It must be the guy at the morgue! When did it happen?" asked Henry.

"Around noon. I saw it on the midday news."

Maddy said, "What if the Whites are storing explosives in the barn?"

"Why would the Whites care about bombing town hall?" asked Emily.

"They didn't have to," said Maddy. "Someone had to make the bomb, right? They could have been testing out explosives near the barn."

Emily said, "And if they did it on an abandoned property, it's better than having the evidence at their own farm."

Henry sat down at the table. "The man in the morgue, Ransom Harris? I wonder if we can link him to the Whites?"

Emily sat down. "What if the Whites are in the business of making explosives? Ruth surely would've put a stop to them trespassing on her property and if she figured out what they were up to she surely would've turned them into the police. And Dan White drives a Tesla. Those cost a pretty penny."

"A clandestine explosives business as motive for murder?" said Henry.

Emily said, "We also need to find out what was on the agenda for the town hall meeting today. What was the purpose of bombing the meeting?"

"I'm up for a bit of research after dinner," said Henry.

"And I want to help," said Maddy.

Henry said, "The whole bomb connection is a bit of a stretch. Besides, I saw this last summer. A young boy with asthma was brought into the ER last summer with breathing issues and it turned out to be the insecticides his father was using."

Emily said, "I know they've been spraying for mosquitos this week."

Maddy, holding her phone, said, "No they weren't. I just went on the town website. This week's spraying has been postponed."

Chapter 10

~

The next day, Henry wasn't scheduled to work so he took a long walk with Spunky while Emily went for a run. He passed Kurt's rental cabin and noticed the white van and pickup truck in the driveway. When Buzz Gordon came out, Henry instinctively ducked behind a cluster of trees with Spunky. He was close enough to hear Buzz talking on his phone.

"I'll deliver right on time. No, yesterday didn't get us off schedule. Right. I'll be there." Buzz hopped into the van and drove off.

"Well, Spunky boy. What do you think that was all about? Deliver what? He mentioned yesterday." Spunky barked and wagged his tail. "Come on, boy. Let's get home."

Emily had just gotten out of the shower. "That was a long walk."

"Yeah. I saw Buzz Gordon. You told me he was renting Kurt's cabin. He was outside on his phone talking about making a delivery. He mentioned something about yesterday not holding him up. Do you think he was referring to explosives in the barn?"

"I don't know. I found the agenda for the town hall meeting after you fell asleep last night." Emily poured herself a cup of coffee.

"What did they discuss? Or did the bombing happen before the meeting?"

"They'd finished the meeting. Thank God no one was seriously injured."

"A man is dead."

"You're right. I should have said no innocent victims were hurt."

"Do you have a copy of the agenda?"

"Yes. The agenda included increasing fines for possession of illegal fireworks, replacing the current recycling contract, and amending zoning laws."

"Amending zoning laws?"

"Specifically, allowing medical facilities and related businesses to open in residential zones. And preventing isolated businesses from opening in commercial zones."

"That doesn't make sense. Businesses by nature are commercial."

"Yes, but for example, adult entertainment establishments can be limited to certain geographic areas. Also, certain businesses have to be a given distance away from schools or churches."

"You know this, how?" Henry folded his arms, partly impressed, partly surprised that she knew this specific information since neither of them had ever considered opening a business.

"Google. Last night."

Henry poured food for both Chester and Spunky before sitting down with a bowl of cereal. "So whoever set off the bomb was concerned with fireworks or zoning laws?"

"Dan and Nan White didn't want Ruth to open a hospital or a 'halfway house' next to their property. Coralee told me as much."

Henry said, "Seems like the current law would have been in their favor. They wouldn't want an amendment. And how does the bomber fit into this? Did he have a stake in seeing the laws amended? What time did you say the bombing happened?"

"Around noon."

"I saw both Nan and Dan earlier than that."

Emily said, "I wish we could get more info on the bomber. I'd like to know if he had a connection to the Whites."

"Like a business transaction involving explosives?" Henry poured a second bowl of cereal.

"I'm going to stroll over to Rebecca and Abby's later. Rebecca knows how to find all kinds of info with her technology knowhow."

"Good idea." Henry's phone buzzed. "It's Pat."

"Take it. I'm going upstairs to dry my hair."

"Hey, Pat. Everything okay?"

"Yeah. I got the lab results back. I wanted to touch base with you on Ransom Harris. The burns were caused by compressed gas. Like a homemade pipe bomb exploded on him."

"So he was the bomber. It fits the timeline, right?"

"Sure does. And Megan said they caught his car on CCTV in the area shortly before the incident."

"That was quick."

"It helps to be married to one of the lead detectives on the case."

"Did next of kin show up? Or did they find out who dumped him at the hospital?"

"No. Megan said they haven't yet found any relatives. He was ex-military."

"So maybe he was trained in explosives?"

"Obviously not well trained. From what Megan told me it was an amateurish job. Hey, I gotta go. Catch you tomorrow."

Henry went upstairs and Emily turned off the blow dryer when she noticed him. "What did he say?"

"The guy in the morgue was ex-military. His car was spotted in the vicinity of town hall around the time of the bombing. They haven't located next of kin."

Emily glanced at the clock on the nightstand. "I'm going over to talk to Rebecca. She's up by now. Want to come?"

"Sure."

They knocked on Abby and Rebecca's door and heard Milo, their Border Collie, barking. Abby answered, camera around her neck and tripod under her arm. "Hi. I'm heading out for a shoot, but come on in. Can I get you something?"

Emily reached down to pet Milo. Rebecca and Abby had done wonders making their cabin homey with quilted pillows and framed landscapes Abby had shot. Vanilla scent emanated from a Yankee Candle on the coffee table. She loved candles, but with Chester and now Spunky running around, she felt she'd be tempting fate. Milo didn't seem to bother with it.

Emily said, "We were hoping to talk to Rebecca. We need her expertise."

Rebecca, dark hair in a braid and wearing a Yale t-shirt, came into the living room. "I thought I heard voices."

Abby said, "I've got to run. Emily and Henry need your computer skills."

Rebecca worked for a company called Biztech and Emily often joked about what kind of tech biz it was. She suspected Rebecca did some high caliber cyber spying or surveillance that she couldn't talk about.

Emily said, "Coralee's good friend was killed the other night. I'm sure you heard about it."

"Sure. It was all over the news. Ruth Winchester. The real estate mogul who drove into the lake, right?"

Emily said, "Except her brakes were cut. She was murdered."

"That's awful. Do they know who did it?"

"No, but we're trying to help the investigation along. Ruth Winchester had recently bought the Gordon farm at a foreclosure auction. The previous owner came to my book signing and made a scene about her stealing his land. That same night, he left early and he has some experience working at a mechanic shop."

"So you think he cut the brakes? To get his farm back?"

"Something like that. But why was it so important to him? The farm hadn't been running for some time. And if he had no money, how is he affording to rent Kurt's cabin?"

Henry said, "He's doing some kind of delivery work. And there's a second barn on his old property. Maddy and I went driving by it. A section of the barn was burned like there could've been an explosion inside. And we found evidence Nan White had been on his property."

Emily said, "Putting that aside for now, you heard about the explosion at town hall right?"

"Yeah. You think Ruth's death had something to do with the bomb going off at Town Hall?" asked Rebecca.

Emily said, "If Ruth moved in, she would've possibly noticed an illegal explosives business. The Whites were eager to keep their privacy."

Henry answered. "We have nothing linking Ransom Harris, the man who died setting off the bomb, to the Whites. The Whites got their injuries before the bombing happened. Pat performed the autopsy on Harris. The lab report shows his injuries are consistent with what one might get from a pipe bomb."

Rebecca said, "And what about what you saw on your patients?"

"I tend to think more of a chemical type burn. I thought pesticides. Planes had been scheduled to do mosquito spraying."

"But they stopped spraying mid-week," said Emily.

"Are you sure?"

"Maddy read it on the town website."

Henry paced across the room, thinking. "Maybe the Whites manufactured the bomb and sold it to Harris."

Emily said, "And Buzz Gordon did the delivering in the white van you saw parked outside Kurt's cabin! You said you saw tire tracks at the barn."

"So the motive for Ruth's murder ran deeper than Buzz being angry over her buying his land. Perhaps he was in the bomb making business with the Whites and Ransom Harris was a customer. Killing Ruth was a way to keep the business going. The second barn is way on the edge of the Gordon farm and abuts the White's property."

Rebecca said, "Then what was the motive for targeting town hall?"

Emily said, "They were discussing amending the zoning laws at the meeting yesterday."

Henry said, "But what was Ransom Harris's motive? We've got nothing."

Rebecca got her laptop. "Who should I search for first?"

"Try Dan White," said Emily. "I tried but there were hundreds of Dan Whites turning up in my searches."

"Give me a few minutes."

Emily tapped her foot waiting while Rebecca did her thing. She wanted nothing more than to bring comfort to Coralee by finding Ruth's killer.

Rebecca said, "Looks like Dan White has a record for assault back a few years ago. He has a chemistry degree from St. Edwards."

Emily said, "They offer an agricultural farming degree. One of my students dated someone who was pursing that major."

Henry said, "He must have enough knowledge to work with explosives."

"Can you search Ransom Harris?"

"Ransom Harris? Spelled like it sounds?"

"Yeah."

"Do we know anything else about him?"

Henry said, "He was ex-military. Probably not part of the explosives unit."

"Give me a few minutes."

It didn't take long for Rebecca to gather information. "He had a restraining order against him."

"By who?"

"Stephanie Harris. His wife. She was in the process of divorcing him."

"How do we find her?"

"The last known address was in Pittsburgh. She worked as a stenographer."

Emily said, "We can call her and see if she knows why he'd do such a thing. Do you have a phone number?"

"Not so easy. She seems to have vanished off the face of the Earth. No info on her for the past three years." Rebecca's short nails clicked on the keyboard. "She was suing him for divorce and full custody of their son. They had a court date but she never showed up. My guess is he either killed her, or she feared he was about to. I'll bet she took the kid and ran far away."

Emily said, "The Whites wanted to stop allowing commercial zoning on the property next to their farm. Ironic if they're running their own business on the property."

Henry said, "But they have an alibi. How does Ransom Harris figure into this? Do you think it's related to his disappearing wife?"

Emily said, "I just thought of something. If the Whites knew how to manufacture bombs, why wouldn't they have rigged up Ruth's car with one rather than cutting the brakes?"

"Rebecca, can you access CCTV footage?"

Henry looked at her like she was crazy. "You're asking her the impossible. How can she …"

Rebecca was already on it. Emily said, "Check the cameras around Town Hall. Look out for a white van or red pickup truck. See if Buzz Gordon was in on this."

"Okay. I've got the footage from the bank across the street. Here we are an hour before…half an hour."

"Wait," said Henry. "That black sedan has been circling the area. Can you pick up the plate?"

"Yeah."

"Keep going," said Henry.

"The man in the black sedan pulled into the parking garage. There he is." She fast forwarded. "He's going behind the town hall building. Alone." She opened a new window on the screen. "The black sedan is registered to Ransom Harris!"

"The police already determined that. But no sign of a white van or red pickup truck?"

"No."

Emily shook her head. "Buzz Gordon wasn't there."

"The only suspicious car I see is the one belonging to the bomber."

Emily said, "Can you pull up footage from the inn the night of the book signing?"

Rebecca sighed. "No, I'm afraid the only one who can do that is Coralee herself. I can't access private security footage at that level."

"Too easy for you?" asked Henry.

"Something like that."

Emily sighed. "I'm more confused than ever."

Chapter 11

~

On the walk back home, Emily had an idea. "Let's head over to the inn and ask Coralee if we can see the security footage. I'm sure she'll be happy to share it. Anything to find Ruth's killer. I'll call her and let her know we need it." She called Coralee, who was more than happy to oblige.

"What's Maddy up to today?" Henry asked. "She was asleep when we left."

"Hanging out with her friend Jenna. She asked if I could drop her off at the mall later. Why do you look concerned? She goes to the mall with her friends all the time."

"The outlet mall?"

"No, the little mall here in town. Why?"

"I got an email from her father," said Henry. "I think he's going to try to come here and see her. I'm worried about her being out like that."

"Why didn't you say anything earlier? How could you keep something like that from me?"

"I didn't want to worry you. And when Maddy and I went driving we stopped at the second barn. We heard rustling coming from the woods. I told Maddy it was probably an animal. She thought it was her father. I hate to admit it, but I wondered the same thing."

"The man is a convicted felon. How is he allowed out on the streets? Maybe she shouldn't go."

"I don't want to make her a prisoner in our home. I had a long talk with her."

"So she knows to be careful?" asked Emily.

"She understands how serious this is. She promised never to be out alone, at least for now. Ron Wooster is keeping on top of the situation. He's as worried about Jessica as we are about Maddy. He promised he'd call if that freak came into town, and he's keeping an eye on both girls."

"It is her summer vacation. If she didn't feel comfortable she wouldn't have made plans to go."

"Right. If she's with a friend at all times and in a crowd at the mall, and as long as she keeps her phone with her and her guard up, she should be okay, right?"

"Right." Emily opened the door and found Maddy curled up on the sofa with Chester. Spunky trotted to the door as soon as it opened.

"Maddy, Emily says you have plans to go to the mall this afternoon. We have no indication that your father's in town, but…"

"I know. You already warned me. Jenna asked me to help her pick out shoes to wear to her mother's wedding. I'll stay with her the whole time and keep my phone on."

Emily said, "We're going to the inn. Why don't you call Jenna and tell her we're on the way?"

Henry took Spunky for a short walk, then they dropped off Maddy and went to see Coralee. Coralee was closing lunch service as they arrived and hung her apron on the hook behind the front desk. Emily hugged her. "How are you holding up?"

"Staying busy. Tomorrow I meet with Ruth's lawyer. I haven't been able to connect with Brianna."

Henry said, "Brianna?"

"Ruth's granddaughter. As far as I know, she's the only living heir. Now, you wanted to see the footage, right?"

Henry said, "Yes. Didn't the police ask for the security footage?"

"They went through it but since it only shows the front door and not the parking lot, they didn't find it useful. Come on. Let's look for ourselves. Come into my office."

She led them behind the front desk into her comfy office. They sat on the floral sofa across from a roll-top desk with a framed picture from her son Noah's graduation.

"We know Buzz Gordon was at the inn the night of Ruth's murder, but how about Dan White? That's who we're looking for, right?" asked Coralee.

Emily said, "He has an alibi. He says he was home watching the Red Sox game and his wife, of course, verified it."

Henry said, "Wait a minute. He was watching the Red Sox the night of the book signing?"

"Yeah, why?"

"They were playing at home against the Yankees that night. I wanted to see it myself and set it up to be recorded. It was rained out before the end of the second inning."

Emily said, "So Dan White lied about his alibi. Surprise, surprise."

Coralee took the laptop from her desk and sat between them on the sofa. "Give me a few minutes. Wish we could see the parking lot. I should probably buy a second camera."

They watched person by person enter the inn. Henry kept checking his phone in case Maddy texted him.

Emily said, "That's Buzz Gordon leaving the inn. Can you make the time stamp bigger?"

"Done."

"Freeze it there," said Emily. "He left the inn right after he blew up at Ruth during dessert."

Henry said, "Wait! Look at the skinny guy in the black get up. He's going inside."

Emily said, "Can you fast forward?"

Coralee forwarded the recording.

Emily said, "That's when the party broke up. See, everyone's leaving. I don't see Ruth."

"How long does it take to cut a car's brakes?" said Coralee.

Henry leaned in closer. "I imagine it's quick if you know what you're doing. It's too bad the camera doesn't reach the parking lot. We know Buzz left the inn when we thought he did, but we don't know if he messed up Ruth's car before he left the parking lot. He and the mystery man in the hoodie definitely had the opportunity."

"So did a handful of other guests." Emily sat back into the sofa. Henry checked his phone again.

Emily said, "Buzz didn't have anything with him, like a backpack of tools to cut the brakes, right?"

"But he may have had them in his trunk."

"You know who we don't see? Dan White."

"Henry's right," said Emily. "We don't see Dan White but who is this mystery man?"

Henry looked at the screen "Can you make it larger? That's better. Wait! I saw him. The night of the book signing at the inn."

Emily said, "Inside the inn? Is he one of your guests, Coralee?"

"No. I've never seen him before."

Amy knocked on the partially open door. "Henry and Em & Em. I didn't know you were coming here today."

Emily said, "It wasn't planned. How are you, honey?"

"I finished cleaning the rooms."

Coralee said, "I put lunch in the fridge for you. Go on, you must be starving by now." She turned to Emily. "Your sister is one of the hardest working employees I've ever had."

Amy noticed the screen, frozen to the frame with the mystery man. "Who's that?"

"We don't know."

"I saw him here at the hotel. Up on the second floor."

Emily said, "Are you sure?"

"Yeah. Remember I went to the kitchen for a snack and I told you I saw Ruth Winchester in the hallway?"

"Yes. But Ruth wasn't staying here. Was he talking to Ruth?"

"He was arguing with her. I heard them when I was going up the stairs. He pulled his hood down when he saw me, but I looked at him first."

Emily said, "Did he say anything to you? Do you know which room he came out of?"

"No, sorry."

Coralee said, "I have an idea. Things are quiet so while Amy has her lunch, let's have a snack. I made an apple pie."

Henry said, "You don't have to ask me twice."

While they chatted over apple pie, Emily received a call from Detective Megan.

"I wanted to let you know we confirmed the facts of the town hall bombing. Ransom Harris was solely responsible. We found bomb making supplies at his home. No connection to the Whites."

"And what was his motive?"

"That's still a question mark," said Megan.

"Okay. If he wasn't buying explosives from the Whites there was no business connection to protect, so he had no motive to kill Ruth."

"And there's no evidence that the Whites are making or storing explosives on their property," said Megan. "That was a weak motive in itself based on a few chemical burns and breathing issues."

Henry cleared his throat. "You can blame me for that one."

Emily said, "Maybe there was another angle. The agenda included amending zoning laws. Is there any reason Ransom would've had a motive to stop the changes?"

Megan said, "He wasn't a business owner and had no plans to relocate here as far as we've found. He lives in Boston."

Emily said, "An inside source told me he was on the verge of a nasty divorce and custody battle. Could the bombing be related?"

"An inside source? You mean your tech savvy neighbor?"

"Maybe."

Megan shook her head. "If we could locate his wife, we might get some answers."

"Who attended the town hall meeting?" asked Coralee. "If I were you, I'd start there."

"We've been interviewing the attendees. Hopefully someone knows something," said Megan. "We're handling it. I've got to get back to work."

Emily tucked her phone back into her purse; Henry's phone rang. "It's Maddy. We've got to go. Now."

Chapter 12

~

Emily's heart ticked like a metronome set to presto. Henry clutched the steering wheel.

"What if she...what if he?" Go faster."

Henry, anger surging through his body, zoomed toward the mall. "Keep your eyes open."

"Oh, my God. No!" shouted Emily.

The light flashed yellow. A wooden gate wobbled in the wind. The rumbling of a train could be heard out of the window. Henry weighed whether or not he could make it across the tracks in time.

"Henry, go!"

"What do you want me to do? Try to beat the train? Okay, hang on."

Emily grasped his arm. "No, I'm sorry. I'm just..."

"Worried. We both are."

After the train had passed, she said, "That looks like the end of the train. Come on. What's taking the bar so long to rise?"

Finally, Henry was able to zoom across the tracks to the mall.

"There she is!" said Emily. "With her friend, Jenna in front of the food court entrance."

Henry pulled up and stepped on the brake a little too roughly. His heart pounded in his chest. "Get in. Jenna, do you need a ride?"

"No, my Mom's on the way."

"You're okay here?"

"Yeah. I see her car turning in now."

Feeling Jenna was safe, Henry pulled away from the entrance. "Tell me what happened. Did you call the police?"

Emily said, "We were so worried."

Maddy's voice quivered. "Jenna and I were in the shoe store. I saw him in the window. He looked right at me, then walked away."

Emily said, "Are you sure it was him?"

"I think it was. He was wearing a cap and dark glasses and he was thinner than I remember from seeing him at the prison, but that creepy smile gave me shivers."

"Did Jenna see him, too?" asked Emily.

"No. By the time she turned around he was gone."

"Did he follow you after you left the shoe store?" Henry gripped the steering wheel so hard Emily could see his veins popping out of his forearms.

"I called you from the store. We stayed inside until a few minutes ago when I knew you'd be outside."

"You should've run to the security guard. What if…"

"The important thing is you're okay and you did the right thing staying put and calling us," said Emily.

Henry called Ron Wooster. "Ron, Maddy thinks she spotted him at the mall. Just now. No, she's not hurt. He leered at her but she didn't give him a chance to follow her. A baseball cap and dark glasses. She's pretty sure. You have to tell Jessica. Did you get any info about him entering the state? Okay. I will."

Maddy said, "Did they trace him to Sugarbury Falls?"

"Ron says no, but I'm not convinced. For now, you stay safe at home unless you're with us. Got it?"

Emily looked at Maddy's scared face. "But you can have Jenna or your other friends over any time you like. It's just until we catch him."

Maddy nodded. "What about the Fourth of July barbecue and fireworks?"

Emily said, "We'll all go together, like last year. I'm sure Ron and Megan will be there, too."

By the time they settled in at home, pizza seemed like the best option for dinner and they made it an early night after all the excitement. Neither Henry nor Emily was able to fall asleep.

"Maybe we should get out of town for a while. We can take Maddy and go visit our friends in New York. Susan says we have an open invitation. Or we can go stay with my mother and Drew."

"No. At least here we know Ron is looking out for him. It's about time we install security cameras of our own. Tomorrow, I'll call a few companies."

The next morning, Henry went to the hospital after checking on Maddy. Emily took Spunky for a walk and wound up at Rebecca and Abby's cabin.

"I'm here to bug you again," said Emily.

"No problem. Come in."

"I smell fresh paint. Is Abby painting?"

"Come see." She led Emily into the guest bedroom. Abby was dressed in overalls; drop cloths lined the floor.

"Hi, Emily. What do you think of the color? They call it robin's egg blue. I'm going to put a mural on the wall across from the crib so the baby will have something stimulating to look at."

"I love the color. This is going to look beautiful."

"The crib will go there, the dresser in front of the mural, and the changing table by the window. Do you think the baby will be too squirmy if he or she can look out the window?"

"I don't know. I've never had an infant. When he or she gets to be a teenager, maybe I can give you advice. Or not. You think you've got something figured out, and the next day it doesn't work. Anyway, the nursery is going to be beautiful."

"Hope so. We don't have a baby yet. I've got time to work on it so if it isn't, I can always start over."

"I'll let you get back to work." She followed Rebecca to her office.

"What can I help you with? Did Coralee share the security footage?"

"Yes. We spotted a thin man in a hoodie who was at the inn the night of the signing but didn't go into the dining room and he wasn't on Coralee's guest list."

"You think he might be the killer?"

"It's possible, but at the moment we have too little to go on."

"You want my help finding out who he is?"

"At the moment, I'm hoping you can dig into the town hall meeting roster. Ransom Harris doesn't seem to have any connection to the Whites, but the agenda included a discussion of zoning laws. What if he had a secret reason to kill Ruth? Something related to plans for the property, maybe."

Rebecca started typing. "Town Hall agenda and roster, right?"

"Yes. I know the police are interviewing the attendees but you're so good at digging up information they might not share."

"Well, here we go. The mayor was there, of course. He generally remains neutral on these matters."

"Any lawyers or real estate people?"

"Well, Rita Winters was there. She owns a real estate agency."

"I know who she is. She owns the agency downtown."

"Yes. It says she's been in business nearly forty years and specializes in residential properties and vacation rentals. I don't see any ties to commercial real estate."

"Ransom Harris was involved in a custody battle and a divorce. Any divorce lawyers or child services employees? Maybe he had an entirely different motive for the bombing which isn't related to Ruth's murder."

"There was a tax lawyer."

Emily looked at the list. "This is a dead end. I'm sorry I wasted your time."

"Did they find his wife?"

"No. And they need her to claim the body."

"Sorry I couldn't be more help."

"It was an idea. Maybe the police will find more when they do their interviews."

Spunky barked. "He's such a good dog. I'd forgotten he was here. I hope Milo gets along with the baby."

"He's great with Spunky and with his sweet disposition I imagine they'll be good buddies. Take care, and thanks again."

Emily made a salad and did the crossword puzzle while she ate. After lunch, Coralee called.

"Emily, I met with Ruth's lawyer. She made me her granddaughter's trustee. I'm supposed to decide when she gets possession of the new cabin and if she's responsible enough to trust with her inheritance."

"Ruth really trusted you."

"I'm not comfortable with all this responsibility. I have no idea where Brianna is at the moment and who am I to judge whether or not she's drug free or will remain drug free. I doubt I'd recognize her. She was a kid last time I saw her. And Ruth left instructions for the property. She wants an 'independent living home' a farm co-op run by the residents. I'm supposed to oversee that, too."

"The bit about the private Veteran's hospital was all for show, wasn't it? She didn't decide at the book signing to go ahead and change her plans. It was a done deal."

Coralee shrugged her shoulders. "I don't know why she was being deceptive, but you're right. She'd changed her will weeks ago. It's more in line with her personality. I was wondering if she was slipping mentally when she suddenly announced a change in plans the night of the signing. Ruth was always a meticulous planner."

"In the new will, Brianna is the primary beneficiary. And it designates funds for the establishment of an independent living home."

Emily said, "Maybe she did that for her granddaughter. So she'd have a safety net if she needed it. If she were still alive, Ruth would be living here in the cottage, nearby."

"Coralee said, "That makes sense.""

"Then what was the deal about a VA hospital if this is what she had in mind?" And pretending she'd never heard of an independent living home—she asked all kinds of questions like she'd never heard of the concept."

Coralee said, "Ruth had been seeing a former marine. I'll bet she had him in mind when she came up with the VA hospital. Then she found out he was soaking her for medical expenses unrelated to any military service. That's when she decided she'd had enough and would move here permanently."

"Makes sense. Did you ever meet him?"

Coralee sighed. "No."

"First order of business is to find Brianna, right?"

"Yes. I was thinking of going back to the cottage to see if we missed something. Want to come?"

"I'll be right over."

When they got to the cabin, Coralee stood frozen on the front stoop.

"What's wrong?"

"It doesn't feel right. This was Ruth's place. I feel like we're invading her privacy. I felt it last time, too."

"We're trying to find her granddaughter and make sure her inheritance goes where she'd planned. That's not invading her privacy. It's being a good friend."

"I guess you're right." Coralee's fingers shook as she inserted the key. "Where do we start?"

"Let's see if she made any notes or left any further instructions. She's got piles of folders on the office floor. That's where we found the new will."

"If it was something personal, she'd have written it in her journal. She did her best thinking at night and often woke up and jotted down ideas that came to her."

"Did you find a journal?"

"I wasn't looking for one. Come on. Let's check her bedroom."

Coralee led the way. Emily started by opening the nightstand drawers. Coralee checked the top of the dresser and the overnight bag sitting on the floor.

"I'm not finding anything? You?"

"No." Emily reached behind the nightstand. "Maybe she dropped the journal behind the nightstand in the middle of the night." She came up empty handed.

Coralee pulled down the comforter. Then she reached under the pillows. "There's something behind the headboard." She reached her hand between the headboard and the wall. Emily heard her groan and knew it was a strain. "I can't reach it."

"Let's move the bed away from the wall." Emily motioned for Coralee to grab one end while she jimmied the other.

Coralee said, "I see something." She reached for the leather journal. "This is it!" She began to flip through.

"Find anything?"

"She has a few addresses and phone numbers here under Brianna's name but she crossed them out." She flipped through the journal. "Here's something. It says *Luisa* with an arrow that says *VA hospital pros*. She lists reasons to open it up." She flipped a few more pages. "Then, there's this."

Emily looked over her shoulder. "It looks like a sketch of a house. See how the rooms are divided?"

"It's the Gordon farm. The street sign is visible. There's more on the next page."

Emily looked over her shoulder. "Looks like an addition to what she had previously."

"She drew a floor plan for an indie-support home."

"Because she read about Amy in my book?"

"And because we had an autistic schoolmate when we were growing up."

"Could she be alive? Do you think Ruth planned to house her there?"

"Unfortunately, no. The friend lived with her mother and when the mother died, she lived alone in the house. She wound up starting a fire and dying. Now it all makes sense."

"She must have been planning this for a long time."

"Everything Ruth ever did was calculated. I didn't want to burst your bubble, thinking you and Amy had convinced her to change her plans on a whim, but I suspected her big announcement was all a big show."

"But Luisa said she changed her mind all the time. She'd hired an architect to draw up the Veteran's hospital and everything."

"Maybe she hadn't confided in Luisa yet, though I'm not sure why."

"Luisa had already started working with an architect to build the hospital."

"Well if that was the case, you can see why she hadn't let her in on the change of plans until the last minute."

Chapter 13

~

Henry called to Emily and Maddy, "Are you girls ready yet? I'm getting hungry."

Emily climbed down the ladder from the loft. She wore navy blue shorts with an Old Navy t-shirt that sported an American flag. White Keds topped off the outfit.

"Don't you look patriotic."

"It's July Fourth, my once a year chance to pull out this t-shirt. I should buy you one."

"I'm okay in my polo shirt, thank you." He rubbed his hands together in anticipation. "We're hitting the food trucks, right? Not bringing quinoa along in a Tupperware or anything, right?"

"Nah. Last year they were selling veggie dogs. I'm thinking deep fried Oreos, cotton candy, and apple pie. I'll try to ignore the calorie counts today."

Maddy came in. "Are we supposed to dress up?"

"Dress up? I'm wearing shorts and a t-shirt."

"I mean the whole red, white, and blue thing."

Emily rolled her eyes. "Wear whatever you want. Me, I'm feeling patriotic today."

"Then let's stay home and watch *Hamilton* on the Disney Channel. We can go out later for the fireworks."

Henry said, "I hope you're not worried about your father turning up?"

"Maybe a little. I guess not with everybody around. It's so hot outside."

"We can go for a swim in Lake Pleasant later if it gets too hot. Wear your swimsuit under your clothes. We'll wait."

"No, let's go."

Henry grabbed his keys and told Spunky they'd bring him a treat.

When they got to the lake, the aroma of grilled sausages, kettle corn, and sunscreen filled the air. Jessica and Ron had grabbed a picnic table.

Emily said, "You must have gotten here at dawn to nab a table."

"Pretty much," said Jessica. We came early to spend time in the water. We were waiting for you to eat."

"I love your red, white, and blue hat," said Emily. She looked right at Maddy while she said it and Maddy shook her head.

Ron said, "Megan and Pat are joining us. They went to buy food. You holding up okay, Maddy? There are still no reports of your father being in town."

"Other than my report?" said Maddy.

Ron turned red. "I didn't mean…of course, I believe you."

Megan and Pat came over with plates heaped full of hotdogs, salads, and chips.

Pat said, "I'm glad the Fourth fell on a Saturday this year. Last year I had to work."

Henry said, "Has to be better than celebrating the Fourth in the morgue. Speaking of the morgue, did next of kin ever turn up to pick up Ransom's body?"

"Oh, yeah. We found his wife. She was hiding in plain sight."

"What do you mean?" asked Emily.

"We found the motive for the bombing. His wife had changed her name and was working as a stenographer here in Sugarbury Falls. Guess who took minutes for the meeting the day of the bombing?"

"No way," said Emily. "She's been here all the time?"

"And he managed to track her down. The bombing was all about killing her without it pointing to him. With a bombing, people wouldn't automatically assume it was personal."

Henry said, "Anything on my burn patients?"

Megan said, "We're still investigating the Whites. They may have been innocent of bombing Town Hall, but they're up to something."

"Do you have anything implicating them in Ruth Winchester's death? Privacy as a motive?"

"Not yet, but Ron and I suspect they're hiding something on their property and don't want nosy neighbors next door. A brand new Tesla? No crops or animals to speak of?"

Emily said, "Can't you check it out?"

"Not without a search warrant."

"Buzz Gordon was there for years," added Emily. "Do you think he knew what they were up to?"

"Not the brightest tool in the box," said Ron. "But if he knew about it, chances are he's involved in whatever they're up to. And apparently it isn't bomb production."

Henry said, "I'm going to buy food. Emily? Maddy?" They followed him to the food trucks.

Emily said, "Look, there's Buzz Gordon talking to the mayor. He's handing him a key ring. What do you think that's about?"

"Who cares?" Maddy swatted a mosquito off her hand. "I thought everyone was hungry. Let's get food and sit down."

"I'll catch up with you," said Emily. I want to say hello to Coralee."

Emily got in line next to Coralee who wore a red and white striped sundress. She knew she wouldn't be the only one dressed in the colors of the flag. She whispered in Coralee's ear. "I'm surprised you're actually letting someone else cook for you."

"Keep this between us, but I'm terrible at outdoor grilling. I'd never make it as a short order cook."

"Did you look over any of the stuff we found at the cottage?"

"I tried the phone numbers we found, but still no leads on Brianna."

"I hate to mention it, but maybe you should check with the police departments, hospitals, rehab centers…"

"There's the issue of confidentiality. I'm not a blood relative. Hospitals and treatment centers aren't going to tell me anything."

Coralee ordered a burger; Emily ordered a veggie dog with sauerkraut and mustard and a plain one with a dab of ketchup for Maddy.

Emily spotted Dan and Buzz heading toward the other side of the lake. "Is there parking on the other side of the lake?"

"Yeah, but plenty right here near the food." They walked back toward the picnic table.

"I wonder what Buzz and the mayor were talking about. He handed Buzz a key. And look. The mayor's heading over to the podium platform."

Henry said, "Looks like he's checking to see if the mics are the right height for his speech later."

Coralee said, "You still think Buzz has something to do with Ruth's death?"

Henry said, "I do. He's done mechanic work and the auto parts strewn around his former property make it look like it could be a hobby."

Emily said, "The Gordon property is the only real motive we have. Either revenge over her buying it, or keeping nosy neighbors away. Have you thought of anything else?"

"Well, I hate to think it." Coralee looked down and shook her head. "No, never mind."

"What?"

"If Brianna needs money and resents Ruth for cutting her out of the will…"

"But she didn't. She rewrote the will to include her. Besides, would she know enough to cut Ruth's brakes even if she were in town?"

Coralee laughed. "Growing up a Winchester? I doubt it."

"Come, join us for lunch."

Ron was talking to Maddy when they got back to the table. "We grabbed the mall security footage. Couldn't identify a balding middle-aged white man wearing a baseball cap sneaking into the mall."

"No one fit the description?" said Maddy.

"Too many fit the description! Seriously, the ones we saw on camera weren't alone or didn't come near matching the body type and race. If he is in town, he picked up a few tricks in prison about avoiding cameras."

Jessica said, "I feel so uneasy. Everywhere I go I think I see him. And every time my phone vibrates my hands shake."

Pat said, "Megan, honey, who are you looking at?"

"The kid in the baggy shorts and white t-shirt. I wouldn't expect to see him here."

"Who is he?"

"Jordan Rae. Ron and I were called down to the high school a few months ago. The principal got an anonymous tip he was selling drugs. They'd been having problems with kids coming to class high."

"That's what happens when they go and make it legal," said Coralee. "I voted against it."

Ron said, "Legal or not, those kids are underage and it's not allowed to be sold or smoked near schools."

Maddy said, "I know him. He was in my art class. He's kind of weird—real shy. He's always been nice to me."

Megan said, "We couldn't pin anything on him. I wonder what he's up to. He lives with his father but I don't see him here. And he doesn't seem to be here with friends."

Maddy said, "I don't think he has any friends."

Emily said, "He's going out toward the other side of the lake. I saw Buzz Gordon head that way when I was getting my food."

Henry said, "Enough about Buzz Gordon, murder, and shady teenagers. This is supposed to be a fun, relaxing day."

Ron said, "I'm flying home with Jessica next weekend to meet her family." He squeezed Jessica's hand.

"That's great," said Coralee. "I'm sure they're going to love you."

"I've gotten to know Ron's parents so it's about time he meets mine." She gave him a peck on the cheek.

"I'm hot," said Maddy. Blond strands stuck to her face like paint running down a wall.

Jessica said, "I'm wearing my bathing suit under my clothes. Did you bring yours?"

Maddy looked at Emily who replied, "I put our swim suits in my bag. Figured we might want to hit the water. You're welcome."

"They've got those canoes for rent, right?" said Henry. "Emily and I are going to row around on the lake. Anyone else?"

"Maybe after a swim," said Pat.

"Maddy, stay with Jessica and Ron. I don't want you vulnerable."

Maddy gave him a salute. "Aye, aye, sir."

While the others swam, Henry and Emily rowed around the lake to the other side. Emily sometimes ran here and she noticed few bikers on the path. With the sun setting, shadows from the trees reflected onto the water, disappearing when they got near the shore.

"Henry, look!"

"At what?"

"That's Buzz Gordon's van and he's talking to that kid Megan said was a suspected drug dealer. I'll bet they're doing some sort of a deal."

"So what if they are. We can't very well do anything about it."

"We can tell Megan and Ron."

"It's their day off."

"Look! Buzz is handing him a box from the back of the van. Let's go tell them."

Henry knew he wouldn't win so he compromised. "We row back and tell Megan or Ron, then leave it to them to deal with and go swimming with Maddy before the fireworks."

They rowed back to the dock while Emily kept the van in sight as long as possible. She swatted at the mosquitos attacking her arm. Too bad the spraying had been postponed. They found Megan and Pat in the water and relayed their observation. Emily felt a little guilty watching her get out and dry off. Even worse when Ron followed.

They found Maddy and Jessica in the water and swam a bit before it turned completely dark. They stopped at the slushy stand on their way to the fireworks display area. Jessica was with them. Ron hadn't yet returned.

Emily ran back to the car for the blanket and they staked out a good spot.

Henry said, "This is Spunky's first Fourth. I hope the fireworks don't scare him. I'm sure he'll be able to hear them."

Maddy said, "You could Face Time him."

"Really?"

"Not unless you taught your miracle dog how to use an iPhone. You better not have bought him the latest model either. I'm stuck with the 10."

Emily said, "Look. There's Buzz and that kid over by the set up area. What are they doing there? Were Ron and Megan too late to catch them?"

Before anyone could respond, Megan and Ron appeared.

Emily got up. "Well? Were we right? Didn't you find drugs on them?"

Megan sighed. "No. What they were up to was perfectly legal."

"Buzz was transporting fireworks, legal fireworks, from the distributor to the display area. The town hired him to do it." Ron flopped onto the blanket next to Jessica. "He says he has a whole barn full on his old property. He buys them from a distributor after the holidays for cheap then resells them the following year. That's one of the reasons he didn't want to give up the land. The guy is trying to make a go of things. He did mention a fire in the barn where some of them exploded from the heat."

"And Jordan Rae?"

Megan said, "He was getting the fireworks to the display area from Buzz's van. The town hired him, too. To help with the actual production. They were both simply doing their jobs."

Emily felt heat rush to her face. "I'm so sorry. I ruined your swim for nothing."

"Me too," said Henry. "We shouldn't have jumped to conclusions."

"I told you he was nice," said Maddy.

"Things aren't always how they appear," said Megan. "I'd say he's off the suspect list for Ruth's murder."

"Having a place to store his merchandise seems like an excuse for murder to me," said Emily.

"Ron and I checked out his story. After he stormed out of the book signing, he stopped at the liquor store on his way home. He should've told us that detail when we first interviewed him, but he admits to guzzling beer on his way home and didn't want us to know. The cashier at the store verified his alibi and we have the time of the purchase from his credit card. He's officially in the clear."

Chapter 14

~

Sunday morning. Emily ran, Henry walked Spunky, and Maddy slept. A typical weekend morning. Brunch at the inn was becoming a habit.

When they arrived, Coralee had reserved a table for them.

"I hope your sister is enjoying the weekend with Frances and Drew," said Coralee. "I sure miss her help."

"She was excited about the big parade and craft fair they promised to take her to. It's hard for my mother to let Amy out of her sight for too long. Not that I blame her a bit. They're driving her back tonight."

"If we find Brianna, maybe she'll bring Ruth's plan to fruition. She left money specifically earmarked for construction, left those preliminary plans, and Luisa is already working with Ruth's architect."

Henry said, "It shouldn't take long to get the necessary permits. Construction could get started before the winter sets in."

"And I followed up on the vote at the Town Hall meeting. The zoning law was amended to allow commercial business next to residential property in the case of something for the good of the community."

Coralee said, "The Whites might argue that bringing drug addicts, drunks, and special needs adults into our community does more harm than good."

"With the laws protecting those with disabilities, they wouldn't have a leg to stand on," Henry said. "Do you have blueberry French Toast today?"

"Of course. And I'll pack a to-go portion for Maddy. I'll send over the server with coffee."

Luisa, Ruth's assistant came over. "I saw you over here. Just wanted to say hello."

"Are you eating alone?"

"With Ruth gone, I don't know anyone else in this town. Coralee was gracious enough to let me stay here until I find another job."

"Sit down and join us," said Emily.

"Have you heard any updates on Ruth's case?"

"The man who stood up at the book signing is in the clear. He has an alibi." Emily debated mentioning what they'd found in Ruth's journal.

"The one who claimed she stole his property from him?"

"That'd be the one. Coralee has been trying to find Ruth's granddaughter. Did Ruth ever mention anything that could help us find her? Did you ever meet her?"

"No."

"Did you know about the change in plans? To ax the Veteran's hospital in lieu of an indie-living home? She must have had you help research it, right?"

"She wanted to leave a legacy behind. And get a tax break, to be honest. When I first started working for her, she was searching for ideas. I told her I had a relative, ex-army, who'd died waiting to get an appointment at a VA hospital."

Henry said, "I can imagine. And those hospitals aren't easily accessible if you live in certain areas. I have a patient in that predicament."

"I guess I planted the seed. Then Ruth started dating the marine so she really hooked into the idea of a private VA hospital. I researched property prices and tax laws in several cities. That's around the time Ruth was looking to buy herself a retirement home."

Emily said, "And she decided on Sugarbury Falls."

"Yes, she loved it here. Found it was one of the only places she could totally relax. And, of course, living near her best friend was a big plus. When she was looking at properties, the realtor mentioned the bank auction. That's when Ruth scooped up the Gordon farm."

The server brought food to the table. Henry doused his French Toast in locally made syrup and Emily dug into her veggie omelet.

Emily said, "Coralee told me Ruth had heard about the Gordon property when she was buying the cottage."

"Yeah. She had me check to make sure it was adequate. It wasn't meant to be a huge hospital, just a small private one which she would personally subsidize."

Henry said, "When did she change her mind about the VA hospital?"

"I didn't know she had! Not until the night she announced it at the book signing."

Emily said, "We found her plans in her journal at the cottage."

"Her journal?" said Luisa.

Henry said, "The so called marine—could he have followed her up here?"

"He was ripping mad when she found him out. Left in a big huff when she said she was going to have him arrested. She threatened to go to the police but he warned her he'd leak the whole thing to the media and she'd appear to the world as a fool retiring out of shame."

"Did she lose a lot of money?" asked Emily.

"Not really. Thank God she caught on before he could do too much damage. When he started asking for money to buy a new car and money to pay for medical needs, she got suspicious. She was no fool."

Henry said, "What did he look like? I saw someone here the night she was murdered and we caught him on camera but couldn't get a clear picture of his face."

"He was quite a bit younger than she was. Average looking. Tall and thin."

Henry said, "I saw someone fitting that description."

"Did you see him here at the inn by any chance?" asked Emily.

"Hmm. No."

"But it's possible he came after her?" said Emily. "Maybe he thought he could still blackmail her into giving him money in exchange for not leaking the story."

"I hadn't thought of that, but I can see it." Luisa took a sip of orange juice.

"What was his name?" asked Henry.

"He called himself Baltimore. Baltimore Dubois. I doubt it was his real name."

"This could be the lead we're looking for. Did you mention him to the detectives when they interviewed you?"

"No, I didn't think of it. But if you think it's important..."

"It could be the lead they need to catch Ruth's killer."

"I'll call them right after breakfast. As a matter of fact, I'm going to eat in my room and call them right now." She pushed away from the table and scurried upstairs.

"That's the first real lead we've had since eliminating Buzz Gordon." Emily took a bite of her omelet and washed it down with a sip of orange juice.

"We still have old Nan and Dan on the list as well." Henry savored a bite of French Toast. "Hey, speak of the devils. Isn't that them waiting in line to come in?"

Emily turned around to look over her shoulder at the hostess stand. "It sure is. Do you honestly think they'd kill over getting new neighbors?"

"Dan lied about his alibi. No Red Sox game, remember? And where'd he get money to buy a Tesla?"

"That's a far cry from murder."

The hostess opened the velvet rope, carried two menus, and led the Whites to a table.

Coralee brought out Maddy's French toast in a to-go bag. Emily filled her in on the conversation with Luisa.

Coralee said, "We saw someone fitting that description on the security tape."

"Luisa went upstairs to call the police and tell them what she remembered. If that's Baltimore—Ruth's marine scam artist—we have a new suspect."

"Emily, how will the police track him down? I'm sure he used a false name and I'll bet he's done this sort of thing to other women and gotten away with it."

Henry sopped up the last bit of blueberry with the last bite of French Toast. "That's it. We research scams on rich ladies in the area and maybe track him down through that."

Coralee said, "Great idea. Megan and Ron can get started on it right away. Meanwhile, maybe we overlooked another clue at the cottage. We didn't see the journal the first time we were out there. What do you think?"

"I think when brunch service is over, we take a ride over there."

"What ever happened with the guy who bombed the town hall meeting? I know he's dead, but did they ever uncover a motive?" asked Coralee.

"He had a restraining order against him. His wife ran away, changed her name, and went into hiding with their son."

"Is she still in hiding?"

Emily said, "They ran here, to Sugarbury Falls. She was a stenographer. For the Town Hall."

Henry added, "He found out and set off the bomb to kill her before the custody hearing, but it backfired on him."

Chapter 15

~

Later in the afternoon, Henry and Emily picked up Coralee and rode over to the cottage.

Coralee headed into the kitchen. She froze in the middle of the floor and looked around.

Emily couldn't help noticing her expression. "What's wrong?"

"Someone's been in here."

"Why do you say that? The door was locked, right?" Emily tried the door leading outside from the kitchen. "This one's locked, too."

"Look at the pantry with the accordion doors. I know I closed it last time we were here and it's partly open."

Henry said, "Are you sure you closed it?"

"Yes, I'm a stickler for closing cabinets. Have to be running a kitchen like I do. I'm positive."

Henry said, "I'll check the other side of the house and make sure the windows are locked."

Emily said, "No one else has a key and I didn't see any signs of a break in."

"I feel it in my bones. Perhaps the previous owners held onto a key and came back for something."

Henry returned to the kitchen. "All the windows are locked. No sign of a break in."

Emily said, "Let's focus on finding the information we need. There's a box of accordion files sitting in the living room. I can start going through those. Henry, you can help me."

"I'll go back through the things in the bedroom," said Coralee.

Coralee went into the bedroom and leafed through the address book on the nightstand. She opened the nightstand drawer, found nothing new of interest, and noticed an envelope had fallen on the floor beside the bed. She didn't remember seeing it the other day when she'd been there. Perhaps it fell out of the journal and they'd been too absorbed reading to notice. She took out a typed note. 'I know you set the cops on me and you'd better watch your back. I'm coming after you. B'.

Coralee ran to the living room and showed the note to Henry and Emily. "B must be Baltimore."

Emily read the note. "How'd we miss that? It shows Baltimore wanted revenge. I wonder if Luisa knew Ruth had reported him after all."

"We'll bring this to Ron and Megan now. They can talk to Luisa again if need be."

Coralee said, "I was so stupid. I touched the envelope and the note. What if there were fingerprints and I messed them up?"

Emily said, "It wasn't sent through the mail. Maybe he slipped it under the door. That means he is—or at least that he was—in town. He must have followed her here."

Henry said, "Surely Ruth touched it before you did. It's doubtful they'd have found prints. Besides, we think we know who wrote it. More importantly, where is he now? Was he in town the night of the murder, and does he have an alibi?"

"After we drop the note off at the station, I'd like to consult with Rebecca again. She may be able to track him down."

In the moment of quiet, they heard a car start and take off. Emily ran to the window. Henry opened the front door.

"Did you see anything?"

"Just missed it. Whoever it was sped down the road before I opened the door. Let's stop by the station."

When they got to the station, Megan was getting ready to head home. "Is something wrong? Maddy didn't see her father, did she?"

Emily said, "No, thank God. She's home with the doors locked. Henry even added a lock on her bedroom door for extra security."

Henry said, "We were at Ruth's cottage and Coralee found a note."

Coralee handed it to Megan. "Luisa said Ruth had been seeing this man shortly before moving here but she found out he was a scammer and Ruth broke it off. Only, he was angry that she threatened to tell the police, so he threatened to make the whole story public if she did."

"And that was his motive for murdering her?"

"Maybe she did go to the police and he found out. The B in the note has to be for Baltimore. It makes sense."

"Why didn't Luisa tell me about him earlier?"

Emily said, "She said she'd forgotten about it, but I think she was trying to protect Ruth's reputation."

Henry said, "I saw him at the inn. He's the man from the security footage. The skinny guy in the hoodie. That's how Luisa described him—tall, skinny, and younger than Ruth."

"Okay, I'll get Luisa down here and question her. Does Luisa know Baltimore's last name?"

"Baltimore Dubois. If he's a scam artist and he's done this to other women, I doubt he used his real name. Maybe you can see if there were similar cases."

"I'll follow up on it."

Henry said, "He was at the house when we were there. I heard a car, but by the time I got to the front door, it was gone."

"You didn't see it at all? No description?"

"No. Sorry. He must have parked in the trees. The driveway was empty when we arrived."

Emily said, "He was a marine, or that's what he told Ruth. He was all for her plan to build a VA hospital. She'd promised him a share in it."

Megan said, "I'll take it from here."

After dropping Coralee back at the inn, Henry and Emily went home and found Maddy watching Netflix with Spunky at her feet and Chester on her lap.

"Everything quiet?" asked Henry.

"Very. Did you find any more clues?"

"Yes. We found a threatening note and someone was at the cottage. Henry heard the car pull away."

"I hope they catch whoever did it. Poor Coralee. Ruth was her best friend. I know how I felt when my mother died."

"We've got two top detectives on it. They'll find him."

"Or her." Maddy hugged Chester closer.

"Or them," said Henry. Spunky barked as if in agreement.

Chapter 16

~

Monday a.m.

Henry had gone to the hospital and Emily got in a few frustrating hours trying to come up with an idea for her next book. What if she simply ran out of ideas? Not that money was a problem. They'd both had good jobs in New York before retiring; they had a small inheritance from Henry's parents, and—as it turned out—they both wound up working part time once they moved here. She was afraid she wouldn't be able to live up to her reputation. It even had a name. Imposter Syndrome. The world would find out she really couldn't write at all.

She needed a break. Maybe a walk would do her good. "Come on, Spunky. You get a bonus walk today." As soon as he saw the leash his tail wagged. If she ever doubted a three-legged mutt could be an exercise companion, Spunky had proven her wrong. They'd talked about getting some sort of wheel device or prosthetic when they first brought him home, but he soon showed he didn't need it.

She found herself at Rebecca and Abby's cabin. Abby was in the yard taking photos. When she saw them, she scratched Spunky between the ears.

"Are you here to see Rebecca?"

"Is it that obvious? I swear I love you both."

"She has a very special skill set."

"As do you."

"Yes, but being a photographer doesn't lend itself to solving crimes. Go on in. The front door is unlocked."

Rebecca had also needed a break and was eating a snack at the kitchen island. Milo perked up when he realized Spunky was visiting. The two dogs got along well.

"Whatever you're eating smells delicious."

"Applesauce cake. Fresh out of the oven. Let me get you a slice."

"You don't have to ask twice."

"What can I help you with? Did you look at Coralee's security footage?"

"Yes. That's kind of why I'm here. We spotted a thin man entering the inn the night of the book signing. Henry passed him in the hallway. He didn't come into the dining room, and Coralee said he wasn't a guest. At brunch, Ruth's assistant, Luisa, remembered Ruth had been seeing a man who fit the description. He called himself Baltimore but it's probably an alias. He tried to pull a scam on Ruth but she was too smart. We think he may have done the same to other women."

"Why do you think he's guilty of murder?"

"We found a threatening note at Ruth's cottage and he warned her not to go to the police about him, but she did. And she'd promised him a job at the VA clinic she was planning, which obviously fell through once she caught on to him."

"The name isn't going to help in a search. You said you suspect he did this to other women?"

"It's just a hunch. And he claimed to be ex-military, but we don't know if that's true."

"Finish your cake first. I'm going for seconds while it's still hot."

Emily's eyes fell on a beautiful landscape painting over the fireplace. "That landscape is new, isn't it?"

"Abby painted it last winter but we recently took the time to frame it and hang it up."

"Her business is doing well?"

"She has more work than she can keep up with. Now that she has a reputation as a wedding photographer, she has to turn down work. Especially from May through October. She barely has time for her creative photography right now, but she will once winter rolls in."

"What's that?" Emily pointed at a wicker bassinet in the corner.

"It was mine when I was a baby."

Emily had never seen the shy side of Rebecca, but now she blushed and looked away. After a moment, a smile formed and her eyes glistened.

"What are you hiding? You look like the cat who ate the canary as my mother likes to say."

Rebecca cleared her throat. "Abby and I are going to be parents."

"Really? I know you were hoping to be."

"We were contacted by a birth mother. After talking with us, she decided we were a perfect fit for her baby. I can't wait to spread the news. You're the first to know, other than my parents. My mother dropped off the bassinet the day after we told her about the pregnancy."

Emily slid off the stool and gave her a hug. "Congratulations! That's wonderful."

"We're very excited, to put it mildly."

"If you need a babysitter, I bet Maddy would be thrilled."

"I'll keep that in mind." She slid off the stool. "Now, let's get to work. You think this guy's a serial scammer, so let's look at news stories. How old do you think he is?"

"Not sure. Luisa said he was quite a bit younger than Ruth—tall and skinny."

Rebecca opened her laptop and clicked the keys. "Did this happen in Vermont?"

"No, in New York."

Rebecca's fingers flew over the keyboard. "I'm checking on stories over the past ten years similar to what you told me."

Emily watched her work. She wished her own fingers had been flying like that this morning when she was trying to write.

"Hey, I think I found something."

"What's that?"

"Look at this clip from *60 Minutes*. There's a story about a serial scammer."

Emily's pulse quickened. She looked over Rebecca's shoulder and squinted trying to read. "He met Suzanne Crow on a dating app. I didn't know people in that age group used dating sites."

"You'd be surprised." She scrolled through the article and stopped with a sigh.

"Well? Could it be our guy?"

"No. The FBI apprehended him when he crossed state lines. He's sitting in a jail cell."

Disappointment washed over Emily. *They'd been close*, she thought.

"Let me keep searching." Rebecca clicked the keys. "No, no…"

"We're not going to find him. It's like looking for a needle in a haystack."

"Wait. Here's a news story about a wealthy New Jersey woman and it sounds similar to what you told me. Man claimed to be a retired army corporal."

"Did they catch the guy?"

Emily felt nauseated watching the screen jump while Rebecca rolled through the article. "Not at the time the article came out. This was three years ago. The woman's name is Trudy Merriweather."

Emily felt butterflies in her stomach. "Can you print it?"

"Sure." She continued typing. "Wait. We aren't done yet. Here's a case from a decade ago. Happened in Hartford. Again, a wealthy woman. They met at a yacht club. I'll print it."

"Thanks, Rebecca. You're amazing. Now we know about a case that happened ten years ago in Hartford, and one that occurred three years ago in New Jersey. I walked in with no leads and now I've got two."

"No problem."

"And it's okay to tell Henry and Maddy about the baby?"

"Yes!"

Emily took Spunky home, calling Coralee on the way. "Hey, I'm leaving Rebecca's and guess what."

"What? Did you get a lead?"

"Rebecca found a news article about a woman in Hartford who was scammed by a younger man she met at a yacht club."

"When did it happen?"

"Ten years ago."

"That's so long ago. He could be halfway around the world by now."

"True, but Rebecca found another case. Three years ago. New Jersey."

"Younger man, older rich woman?"

"Yep."

Coralee said, "And they haven't caught him?"

"Nope. Maybe Megan or Ron can call over to Hartford and New Jersey to see if they can get more information."

"Do you think it was Baltimore at the inn that night?"

"Maybe."

"It wasn't anyone on my guest roster, I can tell you that much. An elderly couple had the room next to Luisa's. Why would he be sneaking around my inn if he wasn't up to no good?"

"Let's see if we can connect the dots. Where did he go after leaving New Jersey and before showing up here? Given it's the same person we're talking about."

"Wherever he went, sounds like he didn't stay put for long," said Coralee.

"I have a hunch he went to New York and hooked up with Ruth. Rebecca gave me a phone number for the woman in New Jersey. Should we give it a try?"

"I'm tied up right now doing payroll."

"I'll do it and get back to you. By the way, Rebecca has some good news she said I could share. She and Abby are adopting a baby!"

"Wow! Those two will be great parents. Imagine growing up around Abby's artistic influence, and Rebecca's technical know-how? I'm so happy for them. Think I'll have time to make a baby quilt before then?"

"You always manage to fit in whatever you set your mind to doing. Now, you go back to work and I'll fill in the police."

Emily called and left a message for Megan. Then she took the number Rebecca gave her for the New Jersey woman and punched it into her phone. Her hands shook slightly at the thought of cold calling, but she could always pull out the 'true crime writer' card if she needed to. No answer. Had to leave a message. Frustrating.

Emily heard a crash. Maddy screamed. Spunky started a barking spree. It took her thirty seconds to rush to her daughter's room.

"What happened? Are you okay?" She threw her arms around Maddy like a protective cloak.

Pieces of glass littered the floor in front of the window. "Someone threw a rock into the window. If I'd been sitting at my desk, it would have hit me."

"Did you hear or see anything?"

"No. Not until the rock crashed through the window."

Emily raced to the window and looked out. On the ground, she saw a bouquet of yellow roses. "Close the door and come into the living room. I see something. Stay inside."

Emily raced out the door. In front of Maddy's window, she saw the roses with a card attached. As much as she was dying to read the card, she stayed clear in order to preserve potential finger prints. She raced back inside and grabbed her phone.

Maddy said, "What was it? Who are you calling?"

"I'm calling Ron. There's a bouquet of yellow roses and a card."

"From who?"

"I didn't want to touch them. We'll wait for Ron. There may be prints."

"It's from my father; I know it is."

"If he left prints, they'll be able to match them with his prison records."

"Should I call Jessica and warn her?"

"I'll bet Ron has already done that."

Emily tried to reassure Maddy that she was safe, but in her heart, she ached at the thought of her father being anywhere near. He'd better not dare cross their paths. She never knew Henry to be violent, but she knew he'd tear the man to pieces if he thought Maddy was in danger. Spunky barked at the door. She heard Ron's car pull into the driveway and ran outside.

"Are you and Maddy okay? He didn't come back, did he?"

"No, but he left Maddy a present, the son of a …"

"Show me what he left." He followed Emily to the outside of Maddy's bedroom window.

Maddy was on her heel.

"Yellow roses?" Ron snapped on latex gloves and picked up the card, gently opening the envelope.

"What does it say?" asked Maddy.

"It says, my darling girl, I can't wait to see you." Ron's phone vibrated in his pocket.

"I see you found the roses."

"Who is this?"

"I didn't forget about your girlfriend. You'd better be treating my daughter right. Did Jessie tell you she received a gift?"

Ron's police training kept him from showing emotion in his voice, but Emily saw the tips of his ears turn red as he clenched the phone. "You will keep away from both girls. I'm filing a restraining order within the hour."

"Come now. They're my flesh and blood. I have the right to give my daughters gifts if I want to."

"I'm calling the authorities in Chicago. You shouldn't take your lucky break for granted. Throwing a rock through a window is intention to harm. I'm requesting you be sent back to prison."

Laughter came through the phone loudly enough to be heard by Emily and Maddy.

Emily couldn't contain herself and shouted back. "Stay away from my daughter or you'll be sorry!" She wished she'd have come up with a more specific threat.

"Bye, for now." He made kissing sounds into the phone before the line went dead.

"How dare he," said Emily. "Can you trace the call?"

"I can try." His phone vibrated in his hand.

Maddy said, "He's calling again? What if he doesn't stop?"

"It's just Jessica. Go on inside with your mom."

Emily said, "Come on. I want to call Henry and let him know what's going on."

Ron said, "Jessica, are you okay?"

"No. I went out to get the mail and found yellow roses in front of the door. It was him. He's in town."

"I know. I'm with Emily and Maddy. He was here, too. Was there a note?"

"It said 'hugs and kisses. See you soon.' I'm scared."

"Lock the door and stay inside. I'm going to go by the station with these roses and the card. Hopefully we'll get prints, but we know it's him. He called me."

"What! How did he get your number? He must be watching us."

"We'll catch him. I'm sleeping at your place tonight and every night until he's back in jail."

Chapter 17

~

It was morning. Emily knew she must have fallen asleep at some point, but felt like she'd been up all night.

Henry towel dried his fresh out of the shower hair. "I'm putting in a call to the Chicago authorities. He has to go back to prison. They haven't responded to the letter I sent."

"Ron filed a restraining order."

"You think that will stop him?"

"Probably not, but if he violates it, he can be arrested, right?"

"If the authorities don't stop him, I will." He threw the towel on the bed. "His latest stunt proves he's in town and that isn't going to fly."

"Shush. Maddy's sleeping on the couch."

"I'll call to get the glass replaced. I want bullet proof glass on that window." He buttoned his shirt and slipped into his shoes.

"What time will you be home?"

"Late afternoon unless there's an emergency." He kissed her cheek. "Have a good one. And be careful."

"I always am."

Emily skipped her run and took a quick shower. She was about to go down for breakfast when her phone buzzed. For a moment, she feared it was Maddy's father.

"Is this Emily Fox, the crime writer?"

"Yes."

"It's Mrs. Merriweather. I recognized your name from the message. I've read both your books. Are you working on a story?"

"I am. I want to ask you about an army corporal who scammed you out of money three years ago."

"That's so embarrassing, but yes, it happened."

"Those types are slick. You're not the first to be duped and you won't be the last. Can you describe the man?"

"Heavy set, hard to believe he was military. Dark hair, balding, walked with a limp. He said it was from a war injury. Should have figured it out then. Said he was shot but I don't think they even use guns anymore in wars with all the technology today."

"You said he walked with a limp?"

"Yes."

"Heavy set? I got a description of him being thin."

"Unless he lost a bunch of weight, the man's beer belly made him look like he was ready to pop a baby out any second."

"Any idea where he went after he left you?"

"Should have gone to jail. Nearly wiped out all my savings."

"Did he ever mention family or where he grew up? Maybe a place where he felt comfortable?"

"No. Not that I'd believe it if he did. Full of lies. He had a bit of a southern drawl which he tried to cover up."

"Thanks. If I send you a picture, can you tell me if it's the same man? It's not clear, but maybe you can tell."

"I'd be glad to."

"Look out for an email and give me a call back."

"I sure will. And I'm waiting for your next book. Keep them coming."

After she ended the call, Emily wondered if there was a way to contact the other woman in Hartford. Rebecca had a phone number but it had happened a decade ago so she wasn't hopeful she'd be able to connect. Even if she did, what would she learn that could be of value? Chester meowed for food.

Seeing Maddy awake before noon during the summer was like seeing snow in July. Henry had left for the hospital and Emily wondered if that woke her up, or if she'd had as much trouble sleeping as she had.

"Good morning. I was about to make breakfast. Do you want scrambled eggs?"

"No thanks. I told Amy I'd come to the inn this morning so we could play with the cats in the café. Want to come? If you don't, I'll need a ride."

"Sure. I haven't seen Amy since she got back from her weekend at home. Come, have a bite to eat first. Did you sleep okay on the sofa?"

"I couldn't stop thinking about what happened. I'll never look at yellow roses in the same way ever again."

"Henry's looking into bullet proof glass for your window."

Maddy cracked a smile. "That's how dads are supposed to be. Not icky stalkers who leave love notes for their daughters and throw rocks through their windows."

"Henry won't let anything happen to you. Neither will I."

"Hey, can I drive to the inn? I need the practice."

Emily swallowed hard...though about her beautiful Audi...and said, "Sure. We'll go nice and slow."

After a jerky ride and glad she hadn't eaten too much for breakfast, Emily gave Maddy a brief lesson on parking. When they got inside, Coralee was on the phone at the front desk. Emily gave her a wave, then followed Maddy upstairs to the cat café, Maddy's school service project. Over a dozen cats had been adopted since it opened her freshman year. Amy poured fresh litter into one of the litter boxes.

"Em & Em. Did you come to play with the cats?"

"I came to see you. How was your Fourth of July back home?"

"Snoopy was scared of the fireworks. He hid under the table. Dorian learned to say 'boom boom.' I taught it to her."

"I'll bet Mom was happy about that."

"Not really. Whenever the microwave dings or the phone rings, Dorian says 'boom boom.' Mom said it's getting on her nerves."

"And that was after one day. Did you enjoy the parade?"

"I did. Emily, I don't want to go back and live with Mom and Drew after the summer is over."

"I'll bet Coralee will keep you on through fall foliage season. The inn's even busier in the fall than it is in the summer."

"I want to stay here."

"At the inn? You don't want to live in one tiny room all the time, do you?"

"I want my own house. I want to live with Dorian and Snoopy."

Emily's heart clenched. She couldn't imagine Amy living on her own. For one thing, she was scared of the dark and would have trouble sleeping in a house all by herself. She didn't know how to cook or pay bills and without a job, who would pay her rent? She and Henry could help a little but once Maddy went to college and they had to cover tuition it would be a whole different story.

Maddy said, "Your mother had to live without you for so many years. She'd be too sad to see you go."

Amy picked up an orange tabby and nuzzled him into her shoulder. She had an affinity for animals and a gentleness that made Emily both happy and sad. The same tenderness that the animals returned, wasn't always the way people responded and she knew how much it hurt Amy to be treated cruelly.

Ironically, her kidnapper—crazy Poppy—had treated her kindly and protected her all those years in spite of living with an arsenal of weapons and thinking he was being stalked by guerillas. Thank God for small miracles. Maybe Ruth's plan could ultimately come to fruition and Amy could live in a home with her peers and work on the farm.

Maddy said, "Where's Stripey?"

"A lady came and adopted her yesterday."

"Another success story," said Emily. Her phone vibrated and she walked over to the corner.

"Ms. Merriweather?"

"Yes. I wanted to tell you I received the photo you sent and it doesn't look at all like the man who scammed me. The body type is all wrong."

"You're sure it can't be him? Even if he'd lost weight? The picture isn't clear."

"It's not him. I'm positive. I'm sorry it isn't what you were hoping to hear."

"Okay. It's helpful knowing for sure. Thanks for calling me back."

"Amy, which is Luisa's room?"

"The one closest to the stairs."

"I'll be right back."

She knocked on the door hoping Luisa hadn't gone into town or out for a walk. She hadn't.

Luisa had her black hair pulled into a high pony tail and wore plastic framed glasses. Emily had only seen her wearing her contacts and with the glasses and no makeup, she looked much older.

"Emily? Do you have news about Ruth?"

"No, but I feel like we're getting closer." She opened her phone. "Is this the man who called himself Baltimore? The one who scammed Ruth?"

Luisa looked at the picture on the phone and immediately answered, "That's not him."

"Look closely."

"I've never seen the man in the photo before."

"You're sure?"

"Positive."

"Did you see a skinny man wearing a hoodie that night? Up here in the hallway?"

"No, I never talked to him or anyone else up here."

Amy came out of the cat café. "There was a skinny man up here. I heard him talking to you. And I heard arguing."

"Talking to me? Wait, there was a handy man here who changed the hall light. Maybe he argued with another guest. It was rather late to be clinking around the hall with a noisy tool box. There's an older couple in the room right there." She pointed at the door next to her room.

"Amy, you said you saw Ruth up here that night. Maybe she argued with him."

"Luisa said, "Ruth went right home after the book signing. Maybe Amy saw the woman next door arguing with the handyman."

Emily knocked on the door. "Hello, I was wondering if I could speak to you for a moment." She knocked again.

Amy said, "I don't think she's there."

Emily said, "I'll try again later. If it wasn't Baltimore, it could have been the skinny guy from the security tape that Henry saw the night of the book signing. But who is he and why was he sneaking around at the inn the night of the murder?"

Amy said, "He didn't change the light bulb. Watch." She stamped on the floor and the light flickered. Emily didn't think it proved anything. After all, it was more likely a problem with the fixture than with the bulb itself. "Can we go back to the cats now?"

"Sure. Come on."

Henry's morning started slowly but by lunch time things picked up at the hospital. He was surprised to see Dan White again.

"What's going on? A problem with the arm? It didn't get infected did it?"

"No, no." Dan coughed as though he had gravel in his chest. "I'm having trouble breathing and I can't shake this cough."

Henry checked the arm to make sure it was healing properly, then listened to Dan's chest. "Take a deep breath."

When he took a breath, Dan went on a coughing jag. "Can I have water?"

Henry called to the nurse and asked her to bring water. "I want to get an x-ray to see what's going on. Any fever? Runny nose? Headache?"

"No, just this cough."

Henry wrote a script. "Take the elevator up one floor and you'll see the imaging lab. I'll call up and let them know you're on the way."

"Thanks, Doc." Dan left and Henry called radiology to give them a heads up.

The radiologist said, "Dr. Fox, while I have you on the phone, I'm having a problem reading a film we took yesterday. Would you mind dropping by and having a look?"

Radiology was Henry's field before he semi-retired. Sugarbury Falls General had desperately needed help in the emergency department when he and Emily first arrived, so he'd agreed to work part time. "I'll be right there."

When he got off the elevator, Dan White was huddled near the window with his phone, speaking rather loudly. The cell reception was notoriously bad in certain spots in the hospital. He was about to tell him the lab was the other way, but stopped to listen to the conversation.

"Drive behind the Gordon property. The access road. There's a barn. No neighbors, we took care of that. I'll meet you there tonight at midnight. Cash only."

Henry ducked around the corner. Dan was describing the barn where he'd taken Maddy driving. Nothing good happens at midnight. Nothing involving cash and an abandoned barn.

Chapter 18

~

When Henry got home later that day, he took Emily with him to walk Spunky.

"I didn't want Maddy to hear, but Dan White came into the ED again today. He was coughing severely and I sent him for an x-ray. I overheard him talking on the phone. Something about a meeting at the Gordon barn at midnight."

"Did you call Megan or Ron?"

"And say what? I eavesdropped on a private phone conversation and heard Dan planning a rendezvous. They'd think I was nuts."

"If something is going down, it may relate to Ruth's murder. Remember, he was big on keeping privacy. If it's something big enough to cause him to kill Ruth…"

"You're jumping the gun, here." Henry nudged Spunky out of a patch of poison ivy.

"The obvious choice is drugs. With all that land, he'd have the room to cultivate pot. And he has an agricultural chemistry degree."

"It's legal now. He doesn't need to sneak around."

"What about the junkers and car parts? Maybe he's got a chop shop going."

"Buzz was the one puttering with cars. Dan White has an electric car. Besides, I've not heard a single word about car thefts in Sugarbury Falls." He stopped at the next tree so Spunky could do his thing. With only three legs, the dog didn't have to lift one and easily marked every tree and mailbox along the way.

"We ruled out bombs and illegal fireworks. I think we should go out there tonight."

"To the Gordon's back barn? It's too dangerous."

"We'd hide in the trees. I'll bring the binoculars. We can even stay in the car if you're worried."

"I don't know. I don't want to leave Maddy alone in the middle of the night. Especially after the roses and broken window. Did the repair man come to fix the glass?"

"Yes, but bullet proof was out of the question. Expensive and we'd have to wait weeks. Maddy's sleeping over at Brooke's house tonight."

"We'd have to keep a good distance away and be ready to zoom out of there if anyone catches sight of us."

"Done."

"We want to find something to entice the police to investigate further. Maybe we'll recognize whoever he's meeting, or we can get a description and maybe a car description and plate number."

"And we'll be super careful."

Spunky tugged on the leash. "Let's get this boy home."

When they got home, Emily grilled a chicken breast for Henry in the George Forman, and microwaved a veggie burger for Maddy and herself. Henry let Maddy practice driving on the way to her friend's house. The afternoon flew by.

After dinner, they tried to watch a movie, but both were too nervous to concentrate. They had helped to solve other murders over the past few years, but from a distance. This time, they were getting up close and personal staking out an abandoned barn on a hidden access road at night. Henry climbed down the ladder.

Emily held back a laugh. "Why are you dressed in black? You look like a Ninja."

"We want to be inconspicuous, right? You should change out of that yellow top."

"I thought we were staying in the car?"

Henry didn't answer. Instead, he checked his watch. "Let's go. The last thing I want is to drive up while this meeting is in progress and have us be spotted."

The further they got from their neighborhood, the darker it became. Street lights were practically nonexistent outside of the down town area. Emily rarely went out this late. The cabins they passed were asleep at this hour and an eerie shiver darted over her.

Henry said, "I'm going to park here. Can you see the area behind the barn with the binoculars?"

She turned on the car's interior light. "Yes. So far, no one is there."

"Turn off the light! It's early. Keep watching."

They took turns with the binoculars. Emily was beginning to think no one would show when Henry said, "I see a car. A man is getting out."

She put her nose to the car window but couldn't see anything but the glare of headlights. "Is Dan out there?"

"Yes. He's carrying something under his arm."

"A gun?"

"No. One of those mailing envelopes. Someone's getting out of the car. Now Dan is opening the envelope to show the guy."

"Now, what?"

"He's shaking his head. Now, the man is pulling out a wad of cash. He's giving it to Dan."

He handed Emily the binoculars. "The man looks barely older than a high school kid. He's taller than Dan, wearing jeans and a red t-shirt. He's getting into a silver something."

Henry took back the binoculars. "It's a silver Infinity. There's mud covering the plate number. He's leaving." Dan disappeared into the barn; the Infinity disappeared down the road.

"Should we wait? If Dan's in the barn, he'll hear us start the car."

They waited thirty minutes, but no sign of Dan.

Henry said, "Wait here. I'm going to peek in the barn and see what he's up to."

"I'll come with you."

"No. If I don't come back in ten minutes, call the police."

"Be careful."

Henry gently shut the car door and jogged over to the barn. He scooted along the barn wall to where he could peer inside. A sliver of moonlight was the only light. He couldn't see much. He listened. Nothing. No sound, no movement. Where did Dan disappear to?

He peeked into the crack in the doors and saw…nothing. Heard nothing. Realizing it was getting to be ten minutes, he jogged back to the car.

"Well? What's he up to in there?"

"He isn't in there. Did you see him sneak out?"

"No. He has to be in there."

"I swear he's not."

"He couldn't vanish into thin air. It's impossible."

"Impossible or not, he's not in there."

"The man in the car gave Dan money. What did he buy from Dan?"

"I wish we knew."

"It had to be valuable enough to keep it private. And possibly to kill Ruth over."

Henry started the car. "Let's go home and try to get a few hours of sleep. I have to be at the hospital for a few hours in the morning."

Chapter 19

~

With Henry at the hospital and Maddy still at Brooke's house, Emily went out for a leisurely run. What was in the envelope Dan had exchanged for the cash? And how did they miss him leaving the barn? Why didn't he do the exchange on his own property?

She leaned on a tree to stretch and was surprised to see Buzz Gordon walking toward the lake with a fishing pole. The path was narrow and she couldn't help but acknowledge him.

"Mr. Gordon. Going fishing?"

"Does it look like I'm going bear hunting? What gave it away?"

"I'm…"

"Used to have a pond right on my own property but you know how that worked out. Hope the druggies know how to fish."

"I'm sorry you were misplaced. I'm sure you'll find another home before long."

"I have the money, you know. I was going to pay off what I owed. Do you know who owns the land now that Ruth Winchester is dead? I was thinking maybe they'd be interested in selling."

"Ruth Winchester had specific plans for the property. She stated in her will she wanted it to be used to build an independent living home."

He mumbled under his breath, but underestimated Emily's keen ears. "There goes my passive income."

"Passive income?"

"Never mind."

"Did you rent out some of the property?" She knew she was coming across as nosy but her former career as a reporter was hard to keep under wraps.

"Something like that."

"Did the Whites rent a portion of your property?"

"I gotta go." He swung the fishing pole over his shoulder and walked away.

Emily thought about it while she ran. The pickup location for last night's exchange was on the Gordon property. Dan White had disappeared into Buzz Gordon's back barn. An underground tunnel played into a mystery she'd helped solve when they first moved to Vermont. What if there was a hidden tunnel connecting the barn to…something on the White's property? The Gordon property had a well-hidden back lot line. The White's abutted a residential street. If they wanted to hide 'business' exchanges like last night, they'd have privacy. Is that what they were renting from Buzz? His back barn? Hidden access to the property?

She finished her lap around the lake and walked to cool down. There was one way to find out and it involved checking out the back barn to see if she was right.

She pulled her phone from her running belt and called Henry. No answer, which meant the ED was busy. Or, he was chatting with Pat down in the morgue and couldn't get a signal.

She called Coralee.

"Hi, Emily. Not too busy on a weekday but it's early yet. Amy's handling the hostess station."

"I have a theory. I think the Whites are renting out Buzz Gordon's back barn and I think there's some sort of underground tunnel connecting it to whatever he's up to on his own property."

"Like back when Noah was involved and we thought he was a thief."

"Glad we were wrong. Your own son. I can't believe I even thought…"

"It's in the past. Did you talk to the police?"

"At this point it sounds like my imagination. Although, there's a little more to it."

"Like what?"

"Henry and I were out at the barn last night. We saw Dan White exchange a manila envelope for cash. Afterwards, Dan disappeared into the Gordon's back barn. Henry peeked in the barn and he had vanished into thin air. A tunnel is the only explanation I can come up with."

"You want to verify before going to the police, is that what you're saying?"

"Yes. It's a bad idea, right? What if he catches me?"

"Why don't you wait for Henry?"

"I don't want to go later when Maddy's home and Henry's not answering his phone right now." Silence. "Coralee? Are you there?"

"Emily, this might be your opportunity. Talk about coincidences. Dan and Nan just walked in for breakfast. Amy's handing them menus. If you go right now, and be quick…"

"Wow. I'll rush right over."

"And I'll make sure to cook the pancakes over low heat. Take your phone and I'll call you when they leave."

"Thanks, Coralee!"

Emily ran home, grabbed her keys, and took off for the Gordon barn. Her hands trembled as she clutched the wheel of her Audi. Knowing Coralee had her back gave her a bit of confidence.

When she got to the access road, she parked in the trees where she and Henry had been the previous night. She scooted across the grass to the barn. It smelled musty and she felt the heavy air weigh her down. Light came through the hole made by the fireworks mishap. It was too small to fit through. She ran back to her car and grabbed the jack from the trunk. Her sweaty hands slipped as she worked to pry open the hole. She jimmied the jack using her body weight to bear down. The sound of the creaking wood egged her on. Then, the rotting wood gave way and split open. Crouching down, making herself as small as possible, she stepped into the barn.

The dirt floor had indentations where Buzz must have had the crates of fireworks stored before he was forced to move them to a storage unit. She opened the creaky door of one of the stalls and…. A whoosh. The flapping of wings. The cawing of a crow. Her heart nearly stopped in her chest.

When she regained her equilibrium, she kicked hay away from the sides of the stall. No openings there.

She pushed the creaky door of the adjacent stall. Again, nothing. She stared up at the loft.

It wouldn't make sense to go up to the loft in order to enter a tunnel. But...

Her eyes were drawn to the area under the loft ladder. She stepped closer. The dirt was a slightly different color, or so she thought. With the muted light coming in, it could simply be a shadow.

She inched her way closer. She crouched down to look. Something moved. She screamed, leaping back up. It took a minute to catch her breath. A large, fuzzy spider crawled right over her running shoe. She kicked at it, punting it across the dirt, convincing herself it was gone. She hated spiders.

Then, she bent down and brushed away bits of hay and loose dirt from the area, praying the spider didn't have family nearby. Her fingers traced the outline of a trap door. Brushing her hand across, she felt a string. A trap door! She tugged at it but it didn't budge. She pulled with all her might. One, two... it popped open with a thud.

Squinting at the time on her phone, she assured herself the Whites must still be at the inn. Coralee hadn't called to say they'd left. Using the flashlight on her phone, she stepped downward onto an unsteady rung. She should go back home and call the police, but here was a window of opportunity with the Whites knowingly occupied. She might not have that again. Besides, if the tunnel led to the White's home, the police would need a warrant and that would take time.

She climbed backwards down another rung, hearing the wood creak. If the ladder gave way, she could twist an ankle, or worse. She moved on, one rung at a time until she found herself in a tunnel! She was right. Vermont was the first state to abolish slavery and historians documented routes to Canada as part of the underground railroad.

She followed the tunnel until it forked into two directions. Unlike the Robert Frost poem, she chose the more traveled path—the one with footprints visible in the damp dirt.

Smelling the damp earth, she worked her way through the tunnel to a ladder. She checked to be sure Coralee hadn't called, then stepped up one rung at a time, feeling splinters of rough wood under her grip. She managed to keep her balance and aimed the phone's flashlight upward, searching for the outline of a trap door. Yes. She'd found it.

With all her might, maintaining a precarious balance, she pushed up the trapdoor. She lifted herself into a stark, white room. When her eyes adjusted to the brightness and she'd successfully blinked out the bits of dust, she saw metal tables with microscopes, test tubes, clear goggles, and plastic bins. Fluorescent lights lined the ceiling; one of the plastic panels was cracked. It smelled like cleaning chemicals and her nose burned when she inhaled.

She bent down to inspect the table. Bottles of liquid. Pills. Further down, lollipops and hard candies. Expecting cannabis plants, she was surprised not to see any. Then she heard a door squeak open. Dan White. Holding a gun. Pointing at her. Her heart skipped a beat.

"What are you doing on my property?"

"I...I know I'm trespassing. I was at the barn. My friend is executor of the estate so it's technically hers at the moment. I found the trap door and this is where it led."

"You should have minded your own business."

"You have a complete lab down here. What is it you're making? Marijuana is legal here now. Can't imagine why you'd have to hide it."

"Do you see plants? The supply is far below the demand for the legal stuff and it's twice as expensive. I started out trying to grow it—all those stupid government regulations and fees. Tried doing it black market but I got caught. They confiscated my plants and warned they'd be watching and I know they did. Drove past nearly every day trying to catch me. Even saw a helicopter hovering over my corn crop several times. Then I had a better idea. Synthetic cannabis. Now that I've gotten the formula right, I'm going to be rich."

Emily's legs felt like Jell-O. "Why do you need the Gordon barn for this?"

"I can't have them catching me again. The tunnel leads out to the barn which is right on the hidden access road. It's perfect."

"Did Buzz Gordon know what you were up to?"

"He didn't know specifics, but I paid him for use of the barn."

"And now that it was going to be under different ownership…"

"I could have maybe gotten away with using the barn if the old lady had moved in and stayed up at the house, but I heard she wanted to build some sort of commune for druggies and drunks. Not that they wouldn't be good customers, but surely they were going to dig around and discover my operation. Couldn't have that."

"So you cut Ruth Winchester's brakes the night of the book signing."

"What? Cut her brakes? No. I'm not a murderer."

"You lied about your alibi. The Red Sox didn't play the night of the murder. You said you were watching them on TV."

"I knew I'd be a suspect. Maybe I've slit a few tires and burned a shed but that's as far as I'd go. I knew without an alibi the cops would think I did it."

Chapter 20

~

Henry picked at his cuticles. Emily was nowhere to be found and wasn't answering her phone. Her running shoes were missing from the mat in front of the door but she never ran this late in the day. He called Coralee.

"She's not home? It's all my fault."

"What's your fault?"

"I told her Dan and Nan White were at the inn eating and she was going to snoop around the back barn of the Gordon property. I was supposed to warn her but had an emergency and didn't. I figured she'd gone home. What if…"

"She's not here. When did you talk to her?"

"This morning."

While he talked, Henry paced back and forth. His blood pressure felt like a levee about to burst. "Something's wrong or she'd be home by now. I'm going over there."

"Be careful. Maybe you should call the police."

"And get her in trouble for trespassing? No thanks."

He stuck his phone in his pocket and grabbed his keys. On the way to the farm, his mind raced. Emily fell and was unconscious. Emily had car trouble. Or worse. He pounded the gas pedal. A pickup truck pulled out of a driveway, forcing him to slow down. Adrenaline took over. He veered onto the grass, swerved around a giant oak tree, and pulled the Jeep back onto the road. Every minute counted as he sped through the country roads.

Henry parked at the access road and immediately saw Emily's Audi in the spot they'd parked the other night. Racing from his Jeep, he peeked in the window and then pulled open the driver side door. Emily was not there but she'd left her purse on the seat. He dug through and noticed her phone was missing. A blessing that she had it with her, but if she did and was in trouble, why didn't she use it? Or why didn't she answer his calls?

He raced to the back barn. Part of the barn wall had been pried open. The jack was on the ground. Pulse racing, he picked it up out of the dirt. In order to fit, he had to pry the boards further apart. His hands shook and the jack slipped out of his grip twice before he was able to make the opening large enough to get through.

When he went inside, it looked as though it hadn't been used as a barn any time recently, if ever. Then he noticed one of the stall doors was open. Once inside, he carefully inspected the sides of the stall, then the floor. Nothing. He looked up at the loft, went to the ladder, and noticed the trap door underneath.

The door pulled open easily. He spotted a ladder and knew in his gut Emily had gone down it. What if she'd fallen and was lying unconscious?

He grabbed his phone and called the police station. "Megan, it's Henry. I'm in the back barn on the Gordon property. I think Emily is down here. Yes, some sort of tunnel. Call an ambulance. Hurry."

He hung up before she could finish telling him to stay put. Using the flashlight on his phone, he climbed down and followed the tunnel. It seemed to go on for miles. At the fork, he saw footprints in the dirt which he was sure were made by Emily's running shoes.

He came to a door and put his ear against it. He heard voices. Should he wait for the police? He heard Emily's voice and a man yelling at her. Dan White. She was in trouble.

Why hadn't he grabbed the jack and taken it with him? If he went in there unarmed, what good would it do if he had a gun?

In a split second decision, he ran backwards through the tunnel, up the ladder, and into the barn. Tools. There had to be something here he could use. He found a rusty hoe in the corner and tucking it under his arm, raced back through the tunnel.

When he got to the door, he still heard Dan yelling. Bracing himself with the hoe, he burst through the door, surprising Dan White. He ran and with all his might, he swung the hoe across Dan's head. Dan collapsed with a crash onto the floor.

"Henry, I was so scared. I knew you'd find me. Untie me."

Henry quickly undid the ropes, keeping an eye on Dan. He didn't notice a gun right away, then saw it lying under a metal table. He grabbed Emily's hand and pulled her into the tunnel right before Dan moaned.

"Come on. Run for it."

Holding Emily's hand, he pulled her through the tunnel. He heard footsteps closing in. Then closer. They were almost back to the barn.

Dan screamed. "You're not getting out of here!"

Henry raced up the ladder, clutching Emily's hand. Then he lost his grip. Dan pulled Emily's leg, tugging her down the ladder.

"Emily! I'm coming."

"Henry!" Her voice echoed through the tunnel. Henry's pulse echoed in his ears. He gripped the ladder and took a step backwards until he heard…

Sirens. Thank God. Reversing course, he raced to the barn door.

"Megan, Ron. He's got her. Hurry!"

"Who's got her?" asked Megan.

"They're down there. Dan White. Dan White has Emily."

Megan raced down the tunnel. Ron followed. Henry held his breath. What if something happened to Emily? He'd never forgive himself for not holding on tighter or running a little faster. He had to stop himself from chasing after them. He couldn't breathe. Not until he heard what he was praying to hear.

"We've got her!" shouted Megan. "She's safe."

A few minutes later, Megan hoisted Emily up the steps. "Ron has Dan White. We're taking him to the station. Are you okay, Emily? I called an ambulance just in case."

"No, I'm fine. I just want to go home."

"We'll need a statement when you're up to it."

"Dan didn't kill Ruth. Neither did Buzz Gordon. Where are we now?" asked Emily.

Megan said, "We're looking into the con artist, Baltimore Dubois, if that's his real name. And there's the skinny guy in the hoodie who showed up on the security camera."

"And whom Amy and Henry both saw at the inn that night."

Chapter 21

~

Maddy sat at the table across from Emily. She'd gotten up early and made pancakes.

"You didn't have to get up early and make a fuss. I'm fine, really."

"It must have been scary. When you saw the gun, did you think that was the end?"

"Adrenaline took over. My mind raced to think of ways out of the situation. Thank God Henry found me when he did."

"Maybe you and Henry ought to get a gun."

"You know I'm against guns."

"But for your, for our protection. If you'd had a gun in your purse…"

"I didn't have my purse with me. Besides, if you pull a gun on someone, you'd better be willing to follow through. I couldn't do it."

"If your life was in danger, I bet you could. Or if mine was."

Emily understood where Maddy was coming from. "You don't need a gun to keep safe from your father. Look how you handled the mall. Did the right thing, staying in the store and waiting for us. If you want to feel empowered, how about karate classes?"

"I will never be okay with wearing a kimono and going barefoot."

"How about if Megan shows you some techniques? She periodically gives a woman's safety class. I took it when we first moved here. We could invite Jessica over, too."

"You mean like hold your keys between your fingers and keep your phone in your hand set for 911?"

"Yeah. And how to break free if your hands are duct taped. You raise your arms over your head like this, and pull down hard, forcing your elbows against your ribcage."

"Tell you what. If you and Henry buy me a car, I promise to keep the keys in my hand to use as a weapon." Maddy took a swig of orange juice.

"I'm serious."

"I'll look it up on YouTube." She scooped up Chester. "Can you drop me off at the inn? I told Amy she could help me set up the cat tree the pet store donated."

"Sure. I told Coralee I'd help her search for Ruth's granddaughter. She has an inheritance waiting. And property. I hope she follows through with the indie-living home."

"That would be perfect for Amy. I'll bet Coralee would keep her on cleaning rooms even after the summer ends."

"The fall foliage season is right around the corner. Besides, knowing Coralee, she'd find a way to keep Amy on even if the inn were to be empty."

"Can I drive to Coralee's?"

"Um, sure." She put her plate in the dishwasher and the juice back in the fridge. "I'll be ready in a few minutes."

When they got to the inn, Coralee was in the middle of breakfast service. She wiped off her hands on her apron. "Maddy, some of the guests have gotten in the habit of taking their coffee and newspaper upstairs to enjoy with the cats. I moved two old nightstands in there to use as end tables. Maybe when your dad has time, he can build us a proper coffee table."

"I'll ask him. Can I take up a tray of pastries?"

"Sure." Coralee brought over a tray from the dining area. "There's apple cinnamon donuts and blueberry muffins." During the week, a continental breakfast buffet was one of the morning options.

Maddy took the tray. "Thanks. Tell Amy I'm upstairs."

"Emily, look at your sister. She's waiting on the customers like an old pro. Look at that great smile. And she gets the orders right. Doesn't even write them down."

"Maybe she's got a future in the hospitality business. I hope Brianna, when we find her, goes along with Ruth's plan."

"How are you feeling? I heard about what happened yesterday. I'm so sorry. If I'd called you like I said I would…"

"I'm fine. Dan White's in jail. We have yet to see whether or not Nan faces charges. Surely she knew about the business."

"Are they cleared for Ruth's murder?"

"Yeah. Megan texted me this morning. He was in the middle of one of his drug deals the night of Ruth's murder."

Coralee said, "Then Baltimore is the only suspect they have?"

"And the skinny guy on your security footage."

"Did Luisa have any luck finding Brianna?"

"No, not yet. Do you want to check with her while I finish up? She's already been down for breakfast."

"Sure." Emily headed upstairs. She stopped outside Luisa's door, sure she heard talking. She waited a moment, then knocked."

"One second."

It took more than a second, but Luisa came to the door. "Emily? Can I help you with something?"

"I came to see if you've had any luck tracking down Brianna. Did you have company? I thought I heard voices?"

"I was on the phone with my mother. I'm thinking of moving in with her. She's at the age where she could use the company and I could use a place to live."

"No new job prospects?"

"Not yet."

"I don't know where to start with locating Brianna. The phone numbers we found at Ruth's cottage didn't pan out. Can you think of anything at all that could help us? Did Ruth mention the name of a rehab?"

"No. I never met Brianna. Ruth wanted to send a birthday card but I couldn't come up with an address. It's like she vanished."

Emily thought she heard something. "What's that sound? Is someone in the bathroom?"

"No, you can hear everything from next door. The walls are paper thin."

"Did you hear anything the night Ruth was killed? Anything could help."

"I heard shouting."

"Who was shouting?"

"A man and a woman. I think it was the couple next door. Or else it was the handyman arguing with someone in the hall."

"With Ruth?"

"No. Ruth wasn't up here that night."

"Okay. If you remember anything else…"

"I'll let you or Coralee know."

Emily went back to the dining room where Coralee was finishing up. "Where's Amy?"

"She went up to the cat café. Shall we get to work?" Coralee opened the door to her office and Emily plopped down on the sofa.

"I asked Luisa if she knew anything but she says she never met Brianna."

"I'd asked her that, too. I remember Ruth saying something about Brianna attending college. It was a state university. Ruth expressed disappointment that Brianna hadn't opted for, or gotten accepted at, a more prestigious school."

"Which state?"

"New York. Not far from the city. She said something about being able to drive up and meet her for lunch if she wanted to."

"Open your laptop and pull up a list of state universities in New York."

Coralee slowly found the proper keys. "My arthritis is acting up."

"Take your time."

"Here we go." Coralee rubbed her hands together.

"Cross off the ones that are more than an hour or two from where Ruth lived. Surely she wasn't about to drive up to Buffalo or Binghamton for lunch."

"SUNY Purchase and SUNY New Paltz are close to the city, to name a few. I'm sure she said it was a four-year school. Now what?"

Emily had learned a few tricks between working as a reporter earlier in her career and hanging around Rebecca. "We can search public records, or we can go to findmyalums.com. We'll need to know the year."

"I think I can estimate the year. Okay. Here goes."

It wasn't as quick or easy as they'd hoped. They searched for hours, and in the end, found two Brianna Winchesters.

Emily said, "Let's pull up their pictures."

Coralee complied. "Okay, but I haven't seen her in years." She scrolled through the pictures. "One is Asian. This other one must be our Brianna. SUNY New Paltz. Now what?"

"That's not far from Westbrook, where Henry and I lived before we moved here. What was her major? We can search job specific sites. Or try LinkedIn."

"She majored in psychology. She could be working in a broad variety of places."

"You said Ruth was worried because she was in and out of rehab. Maybe we can investigate rehabs in the area as well as those in the city."

"You think she's working as a counselor?" asked Coralee.

"That would be the best case. Of course, she may have been a resident. In that case, the information will be confidential."

"So another dead end." Coralee sighed.

"How about hobbies? It's a long shot, but it's worth a try."

"I have no idea what hobbies she was into. This is hopeless."

"She could have gotten married and has a different name now, or she's doing charity work in Botswana for all we know."

Chapter 22

~

Emily left Maddy at the cat café to help Amy set up the new cat tree. She'd just turned on her car when her phone vibrated on the seat next to her.

"Hello." The voice was feeble. "Is this Emily Fox?"

"Yes. Who's this?"

"You left me a message. About the scam artist, Big Tex."

"Big Tex?" It took her a minute to realize who she meant. "You must be the woman from Hartford. You were scammed ten years ago, correct?"

"That's right. Ida Schwartz. Are you writing a book about him?"

"Possibly." The Ruth Winchester murder was on her mind for her next book and if Baltimore—Big Tex—turned out to be the killer… "I realize it was a long time ago."

"I may be old but my mind is sharp as a tack. I remember him all right. Did the police ever catch him?"

"Not yet. And I think he was involved in a murder after pulling a similar scam here in Vermont."

"Did he pretend to be military? With his fat tukis and limp I couldn't imagine. Though he said the limp was a war injury. He claimed he needed surgery and didn't have insurance. Don't Veterans get insurance for life?"

"Did you give him the money?"

"Yeah. And he took off like a bat out of hell. Walked away with the money I was saving to go on a world cruise. He wanted to come with me, on the cruise by the way. Thought he could pick action figures from each port."

"Action figures?"

"He collected military action figures. He was always on the hunt for them, searching on the internet and second hand stores."

"Military action figures?"

"Especially G.I. Joes. There was one he really wanted to get his hands on. Talked about it like it was the holy grail. A 1963, very rare and worth as much as a small house."

"Seriously? Do you remember any particular trade magazines or internet sites he frequented?"

"No, sorry."

"I'm so happy you called me back. I think this hobby might be a means to track him down. If you remember anything else, please don't hesitate to call. If I do wind up writing about him, you'll get a shout out in the acknowledgements."

Emily hung up and felt a ripple of excitement. It was a place to start. She called Trudy Merriweather.

"This is Emily Fox; we spoke the other day. I have a question for you. Did Baltimore have any special interests or hobbies during the time he was with you?"

"Yes. The overgrown baby collected action figures. Had suitcases full of them."

Ripples of hope crawled over her. "Do you remember anything about how he collected them? Did he trade online? Subscribe to any kind of action figure journal?" That was an oxymoron if she ever heard one.

"He did. It was called the Toys R Us catalog!"

Funny, but not helpful. "Thank you. His hobby could be the means to finding him."

"Can I take the first shot when you find him?"

"I'll put in a good word for you. I'm friends with two detectives." She opened her laptop and searched Facebook groups for action figure collectors. She had a few options to possibly draw him out. First, she could pretend to be an enthusiast and join groups hoping he was in it. Very broad. She could narrow it down to GI Joe collectors.

Or she could try Pinterest. Nah. She doubted a lot of men spent time on Pinterest. There had to be trade magazines that had classified ads for people buying and selling. They must have action figure conferences, too, along the lines of comic-con. She sat down and surfed from one site to the next. She heard the key—Henry had picked up Maddy on his way home from the hospital.

"I didn't realize it was this late," said Emily. Henry gave her a kiss and she explained what she was doing.

Maddy got a granola bar from the kitchen and came over. "What are you trying to do?"

"Make a Facebook page for an action figure collector and find places where GI Joes are traded."

"GI what?"

"A toy soldier. Like a Barbie but for boys." She gave Maddy the same description she'd given Henry.

Maddy nudged her away from the keyboard. "You have to make it look real. Add friends. Where do you want to say you went to college?"

"He was in NY last we know."

"Okay. So how about Rutgers? It's only a state away."

"Say something about having been in the army. And make him not too young." She watched Maddy go to town on the profile.

"Okay, how's this picture?"

"You found a picture of GI Joe! Say how he has some rare ones to sell."

"This isn't the place. But there's a Facebook marketplace and of course, eBay. I'm going to make him an Instagram and Twitter account, too. This is fun."

Henry said, "Why don't you run this by Megan or Ron first? Especially after what you went through."

"Okay. If he makes contact, I'll hand it over to them."

"Do you want to go to Coralee's for dinner?"

Maddy said, "I was there all day."

Henry said, "Suit yourself. You can stay home and microwave a veggie burger."

"I'll come. I'm not crazy about staying here alone."

Spunky's tail wagged as soon as Henry grabbed the leash. "I'm taking old faithful for a walk. Want to ask Pat and Megan to join us for dinner if they're free?"

Emily nodded her head and locked the door behind them. Maddy had plopped down on the sofa with Chester. "Have fun at the cat café?"

"Yeah. You should see the new cat tree. It's three levels high."

"I know you're concerned about your father turning up."

"He's in town. He left me flowers. Do you think he's going to turn around and leave without seeing me? And Jessica?"

"If he tries anything, Ron has the restraining order and can send him right back to jail."

"I hope they send him back to Chicago. I'm going to take a quick shower before we go."

Emily checked the new social media accounts. Nothing yet but she had hopes.

At the inn, Coralee sat them at the corner table near the window. Pat and Megan arrived shortly afterwards.

Emily described her plan to Megan.

"That could work but you have to be careful not to give anything away about your location or real identity. On second thought, I'll put an officer in charge of the accounts."

"Don't waste manpower babysitting social media. If I get any sort of hit, I'll call you right away."

"You'd better," said Megan.

Emily said, "There's Luisa. She's all alone."

Megan said, "Have her join us. It's a big table."

Emily invited Luisa, then spotted Amy.

"Em & Em. Are you here for dinner?"

"Yes. Are you finished for the day? Come eat with us."

They settled in at the table. Luisa said, "Have you found Brianna?"

"No, not yet. We found where she went to college but who knows where she went afterwards."

"Did you check rehab centers?" asked Luisa.

"They won't give out that kind of information."

"Once Ruth had me send a check to a rehab in upstate New York."

Amy said, "I lived in upstate New York. With Poppy."

"Yes," said Luisa. "I read the book. It seems you were well taken care of. Poppy was good to you."

"Yes, but now I'm home with Mom and Emily. And Dorian."

"You must have a nice mom if she's letting you keep a parrot in the house," said Luisa. "Have you tried the pot pie? I eat it every time it's on the menu."

"I have," said Amy. "Coralee let me help her make it for lunch once."

Emily's phone dinged, startling her. "What on Earth..."

Maddy said, "I turned on notifications. I wrote that your man Willy was selling a 1963 GI Joe to the highest bidder. Check it out."

Emily looked at her phone. "There are a dozen friend requests. I suppose I should accept."

"If you want to catch him you should," said Maddy.

Megan said, "Let me look. I'll help you word some posts that can narrow our field down to unmarried, middle-aged men, who like dating older woman."

"But it's not a dating site," said Emily.

"Yes, but I know how to craft posts to filter our pool." She winked, "They taught us that in detective school."

Coralee took their orders and soon brought four pot pies and two baked macaroni and cheese casseroles to the table.

Pat said, "Luisa, where are you from?"

"I grew up in upstate New York. My parents had a little farm where my big brother and I learned the art of growing vegetables—what type of fertilizer to use in the spring and protecting them from frost in the winters. It got cold in the winters."

Megan said, "I have a big brother, too. There's nothing like having a third parent."

"My father taught Jaime and me to fish and hunt. We kept it up after he died as sort of a tribute I guess you'd say," added Luisa.

Henry said, "I'm teaching Maddy how to drive. That'll be my legacy, right Maddy?"

Maddy sighed. "A new car for my next birthday would be a true legacy."

"Boy, things are different today. My own mother never had her own car," said Megan.

Pat said, "And I hear kids spend most of their free time in front of video games."

"Jaime and I used to play tag out in the woods until the sun started setting." Luisa sounded wistful.

Pat cleared his throat. "Megan and I were discussing the merits of a big family." He looked at Emily's wide eyes. "Don't get excited. We're still in the planning stages."

"When Amy was missing all those years I felt like my leg had been cut off."

"But you found me," said Amy. "And we're together again." She put her head on Emily's shoulder.

Luisa said, "Did you miss Poppy after Emily found you? You lived with him for three decades after all."

"No. He went to jail. Then he died. Emily and Mom said he had mental illness."

"Sounds like it. Living in the woods in seclusion for thirty years."

Pat said, "Too bad he didn't get to a counselor or something before it was too late."

Megan said, "It's not easy to find a counselor in rural areas. Not like in the cities."

Luisa scooped out a spoonful of pot pie. "Those poor veterans come back from war and can't get the help they need. The country owes them. Baltimore was a scammer but I liked that he convinced Ruth to establish a VA hospital."

"I hear the waits for appointments can be atrocious," said Emily.

Henry finished chewing. "And I have a patient who can't afford his medications. He served in two wars."

"Too bad she changed her mind." Luisa's cheeks turned red as ripe cherries. "I'm sorry. I didn't mean…I know Amy will benefit from an indie-support home."

Emily said, "I suppose Brianna can do what she wants with the property. If we ever find her."

Chapter 23

~

The next morning, Emily invited Rebecca over for coffee. Rebecca showed up with her laptop and an ultrasound picture.

"The birth mother sent us this. He looks sort of like a tadpole. She says she heard the heart beat and it's nice and strong."

"He? Do you know the sex?"

"Not yet. Abby says she doesn't want to know, but I want to know the minute we're able to so we can start thinking of a name."

They sat down at the table and Emily poured them coffee. "I've got store-bought donuts. Nothing as good as the applesauce cake you served me."

"I need to take it easy on the sweets. I'm hoping to lose twenty pounds before we become parents. I'll have to be in good shape to cope with sleepless nights and eventually chasing a toddler. Then there's baseball games and teaching him to ride a bike."

"You said him again. Are you hoping for a boy?"

"Honestly, I just want a healthy child. Imagine if the kid is born without legs or with a heart defect. Keeps me up nights."

"My mother cried for weeks when she found out her baby had Down Syndrome, but once she set her mind to it, she was determined to do her best for Amy. My father, on the other hand... Even as a child, I could tell he was jealous of all the time my mother spent trying to make Amy normal. It was the beginning of the end for their marriage. When we thought Amy had drowned, it was the last straw."

"Well, Abby and I will take what God gives us and love the child even if he—or she—turns out to have three heads!"

"You and Abby will be great parents. I can't wait to meet this baby. Where does the birth mother live?"

"In California. Otherwise we'd be going to doctor appointments with her. We'll fly out for the birth, of course. Now, what can I help you with?"

"The reading of Ruth Winchester's will is coming up and time is running out for Coralee to locate the granddaughter, Brianna. Otherwise, the estate goes into probate. We figured out what college she went to, but don't know where to go from there."

"What's the last name?"

"Winchester, unless she got married."

"What was the college? What year did she graduate?"

Emily gave her the information she had and Rebecca went to work.

"Ruth was a bigshot in the business world. Let's see if we can find any mention of the granddaughter in the media. And I'll check the licensing data base. She majored in psychology, so there are various hoops you need to go through to work say as a school counselor or at a rehab facility."

Maddy walked into the kitchen, startled to see anyone but Emily at home. She said a quick hello while Rebecca worked, then grabbed a donut and poured a cup of milk to dunk it in. She looked at the ultrasound picture on the table.

"This is their baby?"

Emily nodded her head. "Cute, right?"

"Right now it looks like an alien, but I'm sure when it's fully cooked it'll look better."

Rebecca stopped. "I've got a last known address, and a place of employment."

Emily rubbed her hands together. "That's amazing."

"I said last known. She was living and working in Manhattan. The trail goes cold after that. Here's the last phone number and address."

Emily grabbed her phone and her fingers trembled with excitement as she punched in the numbers. Her spirits sank when she found the number no longer in service.

Spunky, who'd been curled in his bed on the kitchen floor, jumped up and started barking as he ran to the back door.

Emily said, "What is it, boy?"

Maddy said, "He never does that. Something's wrong. I'll bet someone's out in the yard."

Emily peeked out. "I don't see anyone."

"I'm going to let Spunky loose to catch him.

"No! If there is someone, he could hurt Spunky. What if…"

"What if he has a gun? We had that discussion, didn't we?"

Spunky ran around to the front window, then slowed down, confident the coast was clear.

"I'm going to take a look," said Emily. Maddy went to the door. "Stay here."

Rebecca said, "I'll come out with you. I need to head home anyway and work my day job."

They went into the yard. Emily turned off the sprinkler. Rebecca saw it first. "Shoe prints. In the mud."

"Someone was out there. And I think I know who. I'll bet it's Maddy's birth father."

"Call the police. Do you want me to stay until they come?"

"No, he's gone by now."

Emily called Ron Wooster and alerted Henry. Both Ron and Megan came by the house. They took pictures and called to have a mold made of the shoeprint.

"Has he been around Jessica's place?"

"She's been staying with me."

"Can't you arrest him or something?"

"Not without proof. You can't positively say he was in your yard. Not to mention we'd have to find him first."

"But he was trespassing."

"I want to grab him and ship him back to prison as much as you do but we have to make it stick. I've got patrol keeping an eye on the motels in town."

"They did a great job of following him here."

Megan said, "Not to change the subject, but I did get a lead off our social media trap."

"Baltimore answered you?"

"I have no way of knowing who's actually behind those posts, but there are two trade shows to note coming up in the near future. The posts are all buzzing about them."

"Where?"

"One's in Atlantic City. The other's in Manhattan."

"Have you checked your social media?" asked Maddy.

Emily grabbed her phone. "I'll do it now. There's something here! A man wants to buy the 1963 GI Joe I mentioned it in my post."

Megan said, "We're getting somewhere. Let's see what the next few days bring."

Emily said, "There's a big toy conference in Manhattan this weekend. And last known address for Brianna is in Manhattan."

"It does seem like a coincidence."

"I think it's a sign. Henry and I haven't had a weekend away in ages. And I have a voucher for a plane ticket that needs to be used before it expires."

"There's no guarantee Baltimore will be at the conference. And how would you find him?"

"I have a picture."

Megan shook her head. "You can't confront him. It's dangerous."

"I won't confront him. I'll find him and call you right away."

"Ron and I have no authority in New York. As a matter of fact, this is bigger than local police."

Ron said, "I don't think it's a good idea. I'll contact the FBI."

"And this will be a priority? Going to a toy convention to catch a scammer who may or may not turn up? I'm not sure any of his victims filed a report. Besides, I also want to follow up on a lead to find Ruth's granddaughter."

Ron said, "Are you taking Maddy?"

Maddy said, "I don't want to sit in a hotel room while you and Henry play Sherlock Holmes."

Ron cleared his throat. "If you and Henry decide to go away for a few days—and I'm not recommending it—Maddy can stay at my place. I've already got Jessica there."

"Jessica and I could catch up. I haven't spent much time with her this summer."

Emily said, "I'll run this plan by Henry. Thanks, Ron. I'd feel okay leaving Maddy if she's under your watch."

Chapter 24

~

Henry and Emily made their way off the plane, thankful not to have to stand at the baggage claim area. They took their carryon bags and grabbed a taxi.

"It's nice having a weekend away together," said Emily.

Henry put his arm around her. "Maddy will be okay, right?"

"Staying with a detective? I think she'll be fine."

They arrived at the hotel, freshened up, and set about to make a plan.

"Here's the last known address from Rebecca for Brianna. And the convention starts tomorrow."

"So we hang around all day at a toy convention?"

"Megan found out there's a booth specifically dealing with selling and trading. They've advertised having the 1963 one for auction. If we see him, we alert Megan and she'll take it from there."

Henry and Emily had dinner near the hotel. Afterwards, they called Maddy to make sure everything was okay.

"It's great. Jessica gave me a driving lesson. Tonight we're going to make popcorn and watch Netflix."

Emily said, "Driving lesson? Shouldn't the two of you stay in?"

"Ron sat in the backseat. He had fun watching Jessica teach me. Kept teasing her about being nervous and correcting how she told me to do things. It was pretty funny."

"Okay, as long as he was right there with you."

"Jessica wants to find out if there are any more of us out there."

"Any more of you?"

"Our sperm donor didn't only do this twice. He's got other children out there. Jessica thinks we can get together and sue him now that he's a free citizen."

"And how does she plan to find these other children? I'm sure they saw the news story when it broke."

"She says some parents would have kept it a secret that they went this route."

"Don't go putting yourself out there on social media. It will only inspire him to come after you quicker."

"Yes, Emily. I've got to go."

Henry said, "What does she have up her sleeve?"

"Nothing rational. I'm exhausted."

He sat on the bed and rubbed her shoulders. "How about a nice warm shower?"

"For you or me?"

He unbuttoned her shirt. "For both of us."

In the morning, they ate hot sesame bagels dripping with butter at the deli next to the hotel, then hailed a taxi to the convention center. With morning traffic and one way streets, Emily felt they could have walked there faster. The taxi dropped them off in front of a marquee that read, Toy-Kon.

"Look at all these kids. This must be exciting for them."

"Yeah, and look around. Plenty of adults without kids, too."

"They went through security and were given goodie bags and plastic ID tags to wear around their necks. They huddled in a corner before entering.

Henry said, "I've got the booth map and a schedule of presentations."

Emily looked over his shoulder. "There's an auction tonight. Let me see that."

She flipped to the back of the program. "That's it. The 1963 GI Joe is up for auction tonight. It's on display at booth 106." She grabbed a pen from her purse and circled it.

Henry flipped through. "Booth 119 says military action figures. We can check that out. And at 10:00, there's a presentation."

They entered the noisy hall full of booth after booth of toys, action figures, comics, and video games. Emily stopped at a Barbie booth.

"I used to love these when I was a kid. I wonder if Maddy liked dolls. I wish I'd known her when she was growing up."

"She's not exactly a grown up now."

"I know. Maybe one day we'll have grandchildren."

"Let's not push it. She doesn't even have her driver's license yet." Though he was sure it wouldn't be long as she was catching on more quickly than he'd expected.

They moved past the Disney booth where the vendors were dressed as Belle and Pluto. It struck Emily as odd. Why not Belle and the beast or Pluto and Donald Duck? Emily looked at each middle aged man she passed that wasn't holding the hand of a child. There weren't many.

Henry said, "I'm checking out the comic books."

"I never saw the point of comic books."

"That's 'cause you're a girl. Anyway, I'm not sure there is a point, but if you're looking for Baltimore he's more likely to be there than at a Disney booth."

While Henry browsed through comics, Emily came to a Vermont based teddy bear booth. She looked through the lacy clad bears with pearls around their necks, the ones dressed in sports uniforms, and those dressed as various professions. She couldn't resist buying one for Rebecca and Abby's baby.

Henry came up behind her. "Maddy's getting a little old for stuffed animals."

"It's not for her. It's for Rebecca and Abby's baby."

"Good because I already bought this for Maddy." He pulled a Veterinarian Barbie from a bag. "I couldn't resist. She can put it on a shelf in her office one day."

She kissed his cheek. "I'm glad you got the chance to be a father. Maddy's lucky to have you." She pulled out her program. "It's almost time for the military figure demonstration. It's down a few aisles and in the back."

"Onward." They arrived in time to grab the last two folding chairs before the presenter picked up the mic. "Pssst. Over there. Could that be him?"

"It's hard to tell from the back." She peered around the end of the aisle. "Maybe."

The presenter demonstrated the newest models and talked about determining value. Then he mentioned the auction coming that night. He rattled off times for various biddings.

"Look," said Henry. "He's frantically copying down the times. Let's do the same."

"Got it."

The man got up and walked past them. Henry said, "Let me see the photo on your phone." He took the phone and compared the two. "That sure looks like him. We'll come back tonight."

They walked past a crowd of people at a roped entrance. Emily asked one of the people in line what it was.

"It's a virtual reality arcade. There's a maze and you use special heat sensors and light blasting guns to shoot your enemies. Kind of an updated paint ball gun or laser tag."

Henry said, "Sounds like fun."

Emily said, "Yes, but the wait must be over an hour. I'd prefer to eat lunch."

They took a long walk, making their way to Rockefeller Center. They ate at an expensive and crowded café, then took a taxi to the 911 Memorial which neither had seen before.

"This is really sobering. Look at all those names." They made their way down a ramp. "Such senseless deaths." Emily wiped tears from her eyes.

"Imagine what those families live with all these years later." They walked out into the sunlight. "Want to head back to the hotel?"

"Sure. We can check on Maddy, have dinner, and make our way to the auction."

Maddy was having a blast hanging out with Jessica. Ron owned a small motor boat and they'd spent the afternoon out on the water. Reassured that their daughter was safe and happy, they ate dinner and headed back to the convention center.

They spotted Baltimore at the auction seated next to an elderly woman dripping in diamonds. Emily wondered if he'd met her at the convention, but Henry had a point in saying, "What on Earth is a woman like that doing at a toy convention? She must be his next mark."

Baltimore aggressively bid on the rare GI Joe and won. The woman with him wrote the check. Emily said, "I'm calling Megan. I'm sure it's him."

As she said that, Baltimore turned as if he'd heard her. Leaving the old lady behind, he pushed his way through the aisle and out the door.

Emily said, "Hurry, let's follow him."

They followed him and he quickened his pace. The rest of the hall was empty since the vendors had closed up for the evening. They saw him duck into the virtual reality room and in a split second decision, followed him into the pitch dark. A maze had been created with crinkly, black paper dividing the room into paths. Every time they bumped into a wall, it made a sound like Chester's crinkly sounding cat toy.

Twists and turns were felt rather than seen. They listened for Baltimore's footsteps, following the whoosh as he bumped into the walls. Then, it was quiet.

"Where did he go? Do you think he got out?"

Henry said, "Impossible. He'd have had to come past us."

"I can't see a thing. Wait. My phone." She turned on the flashlight and Henry did the same with his. "That's better."

They heard a rustle up ahead. "I think he ran into one of the walls. Over this way."

They played a game of cat and mouse, stopping to listen for rattling dividers or footsteps. Henry spotted Baltimore's light. "He's over there."

They worked their way towards him, then he charged right at them, knocking Emily down and fueling Henry's fire. Henry grabbed at his leg, pulling him onto the ground. "End of the road for you, buddy."

"What do you want with me? Are you trying to steal the GI Joe? I don't have it with me. It's in my friend's purse. And I haven't any money."

Henry said, "That's not what we're after. We know who you are and the scam you've been running over the past decade."

Emily said, "And we know you killed Ruth Winchester."

"Killed Ruth Winchester? Wait a cotton pickin' minute. I may have allegedly persuaded her to part with some funds, but murder? No way."

Henry jammed his knee harder into Baltimore's chest. "We've got you now. The police will be here any minute."

"You can't try and pin murder on me. Ruth Winchester? You're looking in the wrong direction. If you want to find her killer, look at the young lady and her hippy boyfriend. They had more motive than I did."

"What young lady? What boyfriend?"

Lights flooded the tunnel. "FBI. Put your hands where we can see them."

They grabbed Baltimore, took statements from Henry and Emily, and thanked them for helping track him down.

"We've had him on our radar for years but never could catch him. Frankly, there were more urgent cases to deal with. Your friends at the Sugarbury Falls police department alerted us."

"Well, he just purchased a valuable action figure. Perhaps if it's confiscated and sold, those poor widows he took advantage of can get back some of what he stole," said Emily.

Henry said, "He was here with an elderly woman. It's in her purse."

The agents led him away and Emily and Henry went back to the hotel.

Emily said, "Young lady and her boyfriend? Do you think he means Brianna?"

"The man I saw at the inn and we saw on the tape could be described as a hippy."

"But where's Brianna? We didn't see her."

"Let's see what they learn from questioning Baltimore. Of course he's going to deny killing Ruth."

"Yeah. Right now all I want to do is crawl under the covers and go to sleep."

Chapter 25

~

The next morning, Megan called to say Baltimore had an alibi for the night Ruth was killed.

"Are you certain? He could be lying."

Megan said, "He was at a country club having dinner with his next victim. We have him on security video and there are witnesses."

"He said something about a young lady and her hippy boyfriend. That has to be Brianna. Ask him about it."

"I'm not in on this case. The FBI is handling it."

"Can you pass on the information at least?"

"I'll do my best."

Emily put down her phone and sighed. "So much for that theory."

Henry said, "Look at it this way. We didn't find Ruth's killer but we got justice for those poor women he swindled and the future ones he'd have gone after."

"And Baltimore thinks Brianna and her boyfriend killed Ruth."

"He's a known liar. I wouldn't put much stock in it."

"But remember the man on the security tape at Coralee's the night of the murder? You saw him there in the inn. I'll bet it was him."

"The skinny guy in the hoodie. But where was Brianna? No one saw a girl fitting her description."

"Coralee said she had long curly dark hair like Ruth did before she turned gray. But that was some time ago. By now it could be spiked and dyed purple."

"You have an address from Rebecca. After we finish brunch, let's start there."

They went back to the room and checked out directions.

"Looks like our best bet is the subway," said Henry.

"I know it's a long shot, but imagine if we find her there and can bring her to Sugarbury Falls for the will reading."

"I doubt it will be that easy. Come on."

It was less than a thirty-minute train ride to Jackson Heights. They climbed up the subway station stairs into the daylight. Henry looked at the directions and they headed toward the address.

Emily said, "It should be coming up soon." She was sweating in the asphalt magnified city heat.

"Another block." They picked up the pace. Henry checked the building numbers against his phone. "Here we are." He stopped in front of a brick apartment building with white columns supporting an overhang. Window A/C units swelled out of five stories worth of windows.

Emily said, "Let's go in. It doesn't look like there's security."

They walked right through the lobby and up to the second floor where they knocked on the last known address for Brianna. There was no answer.

A woman carrying a laundry basket appeared when the elevator doors opened. She fumbled with a key to the next apartment.

Emily said, "Excuse me. We're looking for Brianna Winchester. This is the address we have for her. Do you happen to know if she still lives here?"

"Brianna? She used to but not for several months now."

"You wouldn't happen to know where she moved to, do you? Her grandmother died and it's important we locate her."

"No. She said something about a new job that provided housing."

"Where had she been working?'

"She worked for the Disabled Veterans. It's around the corner from here. I donated a bunch of clothes for her to take over there."

"Can you tell us anything else? Any clue where she may have gone?"

"She said she couldn't say. Confidentiality or something like that." The neighbor shifted the laundry basket, then gave up and set it on the floor while she opened her door. "Good luck. She was a good neighbor."

Henry said, "Did friends ever come around? Do you know if she had a boyfriend?"

"Not that I ever saw."

They went back outside and talked about their next move.

"We can walk over to the Disabled Vets but it's Sunday. I'm not sure they'll be open," said Henry. "It's this way."

By the time they found the Disabled Vets office, Emily's shirt stuck to her skin and Henry's forehead glistened. The blinds across the front window were closed and they were about to turn around and head to the hotel when someone peeked through the blinds. Henry motioned toward the door. A woman mouthed, "We're closed."

Henry held up a finger. "One minute of your time, please."

They heard the door open and an older woman appeared. She was missing an arm from the elbow down. "All right, come in. I suppose this is some sort of an emergency."

Emily said, "We really appreciate this. We're looking for a woman named Brianna Winchester. Her grandmother recently died and we can't locate her."

"Bri? Black hair, in her late twenties?"

"Yes!" Emily's pulse raced.

"She ain't here."

"But she works here? Will she be back tomorrow?"

"Naw. She quit."

"Quit?"

"Bri was a sweetheart, but she was kind of disillusioned with our whole operation. You know these young people. Come out of college and want to do good for the world—think they can make a difference and all." She laughed. "Then they see the reality."

Emily said, "Aren't you a service organization?"

"Sure, but it takes money to save the world. We turn away far more veterans than we help, I hate to admit. We do our best but it feels like we're riding a surfboard against a tidal wave."

"Brianna quit over that?"

"Do you blame her? People come in here swearing and complaining they can't get help or their family members are let down. Don't blame them but we do what we can with what we've got. She got another offer. Felt she could do more good somewhere else."

"Where?"

"She couldn't say exactly. Something about confidentiality. I thought it was maybe one of those woman's shelters."

Emily said, "Here's my card. Brianna stands to inherit money if we can locate her. If you think of anything…"

"Sure."

Defeated, they got back on the subway and headed to the hotel.

"That was a waste," said Emily. "For a moment, I thought we were close." She opened her small suitcase and began tossing in clothes.

Henry clasped her wrist. "I know you're disappointed. You don't have to pack now. Our flight isn't until tomorrow. We have a whole evening left to enjoy the city."

Emily sat on the bed. "You're right. We did what we could. The will reading is in a few days and whatever happens happens."

They spent the evening going to dinner and enjoying an off Broadway production of *Mousetrap*. In the morning, while they were packing, Emily's phone rang.

"Is this Emily Fox?"

"Yes, it is."

"I heard you were looking for Brianna Winchester. Something about an inheritance?"

"Yes. Do you know her?"

"We're friends. We worked together at the Disabled Vets office. My mother works there too. You spoke with her today."

"Yes. Do you know how to contact her?"

"Yes. But she'll have to come to you. She says she can meet you in Central Park in front of Cleopatra's Needle at noon."

"It's cutting it close…we're flying home today."

"Then I'll tell her it's a no."

"Don't do that. We'll make it work. Noon at Cleopatra's Needle. We'll be there."

Chapter 26

~

"Do you think she'll show up?" said Emily.

"Why wouldn't she. This was her idea."

"It's ten after. We're going to miss out flight if we wait much longer. Let's go."

"Wait. Could that be her?"

A young woman with a dark ponytail in a sundress came toward them. "Are you Emily?"

"Yes. Brianna?"

"That's me. Tell me why you were trying so hard to find me."

Henry said, "Let's sit down." They followed him to a bench. "I hate to bring bad news, but your grandmother has recently died."

"Died? She was the picture of health last I checked. I just returned from vacation and haven't had time to call her. What happened?"

Emily said, "I hate to tell you this, but she was murdered."

"Murdered! By whom?"

"We're trying to find out."

"Are you detectives?"

"Not exactly. We're friends of Ruth's dear friend Coralee. Coralee is executor of the will and you stand to inherit her property."

"Coralee in Sugarbury Falls? Grandma Ruth adored her."

"We hope you can come to the reading. Coralee has been searching for you."

"Of course. But I want to know who killed her. She had some business enemies, but murder?"

"Maybe you can help. The FBI arrested a man named Baltimore Dubois. He tried to swindle your grandmother but she caught on in time. We've ruled out people in town who didn't want her to buy property she'd purchased. When no one could find you…"

"Surely I'm not a suspect. I loved my grandmother."

Emily said, "She hadn't heard from you. She thought maybe you'd…"

"Fallen off the wagon? No way. I've gotten my life together. Besides, we talked every week before I went off on vacation. I'm resident director of a drug rehab facility. I couldn't disclose my address. Several famous people are in treatment at any given time and with confidentiality paramount…"

"Your grandmother had plans to build a veteran's clinic. Then she changed those plans to make it an indie-living facility. Do you know anything about that?"

"Well, I told her first-hand how bad things were for our veterans. She heard it personally from her assistant and her then con man boyfriend."

"Her assistant?"

"There was a woman who came around the disabled vets' office many times. She wanted help for her brother who was in prison. He had mental issues stemming from the Vietnam War and he was being ignored in prison. She was angry and had lost her job in pursuit of seeking help for him. Her brother committed suicide in prison."

"And she worked for your grandmother?"

"I sent her over there. She was trained as a managerial assistant and I knew my grandmother had recently lost hers so it was a win-win."

"Was her name Luisa?"

"Yeah, that's it."

Henry said, "Why did your grandmother change her mind about the veteran's clinic?"

"When she found out about Baltimore, she went ballistic. There was no way she was going to support it. The whole set up was his idea and he was supposed to run it. Then, she happened upon a card from a friend she grew up with whose daughter was mentally impaired. She took it as a sign and changed her plans."

Emily said, "Luisa wouldn't have been angry enough to kill your grandmother, would she?"

"Luisa? I can't imagine it. She really cared about helping the veterans. She didn't strike me as the violent type."

Henry said, "Did she happen to know her way around cars, by any chance?"

Brianna laughed. "Are you kidding? She called a mechanic to replace her windshield wiper fluid. Grandma Ruth thought it was hysterical."

"Did Luisa have a boyfriend?" asked Emily.

"Not that I know of."

Emily looked at her watch. "We've got a flight to catch. The reading of the will is on Wednesday. Can you make it to Sugarbury Falls? It's important."

"Of course. I'll reserve a hotel."

"You don't have to. According to Coralee, you inherit the entire estate, including the new cottage she purchased."

Henry added, "And you own a farm! No animals though. It's where Ruth was going to build the indie-support home. It's up to you to do what you want with it."

"Wow, it's a lot to digest. And I have to arrange a proper funeral. She wanted to be buried next to her daughter—my mother. I can't believe she's gone."

Henry said, "We're sorry for your loss. We'll see you on Wednesday."

They made their flight with minutes to spare. On the plane, they discussed the events of the weekend.

"We still don't know who killed Ruth," said Emily.

"Maybe Brianna was right and it was a business enemy."

"A business enemy followed her to Vermont and messed with her brakes? Now that she was planning to spend less time with her company?"

Henry said, "I suppose they'd have killed her in New York rather than following her to Sugarbury Falls. And messing with the brakes?"

"We did see the skinny guy in the hoodie heading to the parking lot. Do you think he was a disgruntled vet? Or a business enemy?"

"He looked kind of young, but maybe. He had means and opportunity but what was his motive? Ruth changing her mind about the vet clinic? She fired him? And where is he now?" Henry poured the miniature bag of peanuts into his palm and into his mouth.

"What if he's a relative she disinherited?" Emily took a sip of her soda.

"Brianna didn't mention any other relatives. I don't know. We've eliminated those on the list. At least we found Brianna and she'll be at the reading and get what's rightly hers."

Emily said, "I'm going to close my eyes and grab a nap before we land."

"Better hurry. This is a short flight."

When they got back home, Maddy was waiting with Jessica. Spunky nearly knocked Henry over with his enthusiasm.

Henry said, "I bought you a present."

"Bought Spunky a present?"

"No, silly. For you."

Maddy's eyes lit up. "What is it? A car?"

"No." He pulled the Barbie out of his carry-on. "You can keep it on your desk in your office when you become a veterinarian." He pulled the souvenir stress ball out of his carry-on and tossed it to Spunky while Maddy was distracted.

She hugged him. "I used to love Barbie. Thanks. I was only expecting a t-shirt."

Emily turned to Jessica. "Sounds like things have been quiet here."

"Yes. Well, we did make contact with a potential half-sister on social media."

"Jessica, I told Maddy to stay away from doing that. You never know what kind of weirdos might respond and how can you trust they're telling the truth?"

"She knew things that weren't made public. And the timeline fits. But don't worry. It's not like we told her where we live or anything."

"Why?"

"If you had a sister out there somewhere, wouldn't you be curious?"

The thirty years and subsequent search for Amy gave Emily a bit of empathy.

Maddy said, "We went by to see Amy and visit the cat café earlier. Coralee said to tell you to come for dinner. She's trying a recipe for vegetarian pot roast. Don't ask. There's always salad."

"Sounds good. I don't feel like grocery shopping and I'd love to catch her up on our trip. Jessica, why don't you and Ron come too?"

"We've plans tonight. Another time."

Maddy said, "So what was Ruth's granddaughter like? Was she in rehab all this time Coralee was looking for her?"

"No, not at all. She works and lives in a rehab that caters to celebrities so she isn't allowed to disclose the address. Besides, she'd been on vacation the past couple of weeks."

Henry said, "She's coming into town for the reading of the will. You'll have a chance to meet her."

Emily and Henry spent the afternoon unpacking and napping. Henry took Spunky on an extra-long walk and Chester snuggled with Emily. Maddy drove them to the inn for dinner, impressing both her parents with her driving skills.

Coralee greeted them in the lobby. "Glad you could make it. I can't thank you enough for hunting down Brianna. It was weighing heavily on my mind."

"She'll be here for the reading. She certainly seems put together. You'd never guess she struggled with addiction," said Emily.

Luisa came down to the dining area. "I thought I'd pick up dinner to bring back to the room."

Emily said, "Why don't you join us? You must get stir crazy looking at the walls all day."

"Okay. I'm hoping I'll be out soon. I have an interview at the end of the week. Once I know I'll have a paycheck again I can start apartment hunting."

They settled in at a corner table. Emily said, "We found Ruth's granddaughter."

"Really? Is she out of rehab?"

"Yes. She has been for some time. She says she had been in contact with Ruth."

"Hmm."

Emily said, "Brianna says she knows you from the disabled vet's office. You came in to try to get help for your brother and then she got you the job working for Ruth."

Luisa pushed back from the table, mouth half open with surprise. "She said what? That's…that's a total lie. I found the job through an employment agency. We've never met. And I've never set foot in a disabled veteran's office."

Emily tried to digest what she was hearing. "She was lying to us? Why?"

Henry said, "Do you have a brother who fought in Vietnam?"

Luisa said, "No, I don't have a brother. Whatever lies this girl told you aren't true. Are you sure she was Ruth's granddaughter?"

"It's not like we asked to see her driver's license or anything. It didn't occur to us that she'd lie," said Emily. "And what was her motive?"

"That's an easy one. She pretends to be Ruth's granddaughter and walks away with the inheritance."

Chapter 27

~

Emily went for a run in the morning to clear her head. If the woman they met was an imposter, then where was the real Brianna Winchester? Rotting away somewhere? Surely the lawyer would check her identity before handing over Ruth's fortune. She couldn't resist knocking on Rebecca's door.

"I hope it isn't too early."

"No, come on in. Everything okay?"

"Yeah. I need you to do a bit more detective work for me. Can you verify that the girl who claims to be Brianna actually is her?"

"Are you doubting it?"

"We met with her in New York. Lovely girl. It's just some things don't add up. Luisa, Ruth's assistant, says she never met Brianna, yet Brianna tells a whole story about how she met Luisa and got her the job working with Ruth. She seemed to know a lot about Ruth, even knew about Baltimore and Ruth's plans for the VA hospital and how she changed her mind about turning it into an indie-support home."

"Well, let's look at her social media pictures." She clicked a few keys and in record time had a post. "Is this her? In Paris?"

"Yes! She said she just got back from vacation."

"Here's a driver's license. It's the same girl. Of course, we don't know how long she's been impersonating Brianna. That's supposing Luisa is telling the truth."

"Can you find a picture from when she was younger? Wait. I saw some at Ruth's cottage."

"I've got a yearbook picture here. Is this her?"

Emily peeked over her shoulder. "It certainly looks like her. Do you think she has a twin?"

"I doubt it. There's nothing in her social media indicating a twin. She says she's an only child in her profile."

"Can you find anything on Luisa?"

Rebecca searched. "She doesn't have an on-line presence. Do you know her last name?"

"Umm, no. I guess that's not helpful. I can find out."

"Do that and I'm sure I'll be able to help you."

Emily's heart raced. Who was telling the truth, Brianna or Luisa?

Henry had left for the hospital before she got back home. She decided to head over to the inn and have a chat with Luisa. Brianna texted her that she'd be arriving in town later that day.

"Coralee, is Luisa in her room?"

"I didn't see her at breakfast. Go knock on her door."

Emily knocked but no answer. Where would she go?

She went back downstairs. "Coralee, did Luisa give you a name or credit card when she registered?"

"She didn't register. I gave her the room complimentary. Meals too. I think Ruth would have wanted that. Poor girl is out of a job. In fact, she said something about an interview. Perhaps she left early to get to it."

Emily remembered her saying something about an interview. She saw Amy in the dining room.

"Em & Em. What are you doing here?"

"Came by to see Coralee. And you, of course. I was looking for Luisa. Did you see her?"

"Yeah. She left with her boyfriend."

"Boyfriend?"

"The skinny guy with the hoodie."

"The one you saw her with the night of the book signing? The one she said was a handyman?"

"Yeah. She had her suitcase with her, too."

Emily ran to Coralee. "Amy says Luisa left with the hoodie guy. Did she check out? Amy said she had a suitcase."

"She never said she was leaving. How do you like that. Not even a thank you."

"Can you open her room?"

"I suppose so."

She followed Coralee upstairs. Inside, were a few random items left behind. She picked through the wastebasket and found a receipt. Oh my God. It can't be."

"Emily, what's wrong? You're white as a ghost."

Her voice trembled. "I...I've got to go."

Emily jumped into her Audi and almost forgot to release the parking brake before stepping on the gas. Before she got out of the parking lot, her seat belt reminder dinged. She had to get there quickly. She had to see Rebecca.

In record time, she pulled in front of Rebecca and Abby's cabin and slammed on the brakes. She ran to the door, pounding and calling for Rebecca.

"Emily, what's wrong? Is someone hurt?"

"I need your help. Get your computer out. Please."

"Yeah, yeah. Come in." Emily followed on her heel. "I need you to check something."

Rebecca started the laptop. "Shoot."

"I think Luisa is related to Poppy, the man who kidnapped Amy. She has the same last name."

"Lots of people with the same last name aren't related."

Emily's heart wouldn't stop pounding. "Check Luisa Mulvaney."

"Okay. Give me a minute. Do you have an approximate age? Occupation?"

"She's a trained as a secretary. I'd say mid to late 40's."

"What do you want to know?"

"Was she married to or related to Poppy Mulvaney?" Seconds seemed like hours as she waited.

"She has an older brother named George. Deceased. He fought in Vietnam, lived in New York ..."

"That's got to be him. That's the connection." A text arrived. "It's Brianna. She landed and is on the way to Ruth's cottage." She texted back. "I'll meet you there."

"There's a connection between Luisa and the man who kidnapped Amy. Brother and sister. If Brianna was telling the truth, and I'm inclined to think she is, Luisa had a passion for the cause of getting benefits for disabled veterans. Her brother died unable to get help. She must have been thrilled when Ruth planned the VA hospital and devastated when she changed her mind."

"You don't think she killed Ruth, do you?"

"Of course she did. Why else would she lie? What if she was so upset by Ruth withdrawing her plans for the VA hospital that she killed her?"

"I'm sure she was upset, but upset enough to kill over? That's hard to believe," said Rebecca.

"I found papers in her hotel room. It looked like an amended copy of Ruth's will. Here." She pulled it from her purse. "This isn't the same will I saw at Ruth's cottage. Which one does the lawyer have? I have to retrieve Ruth's copy from the cottage."

"It's a will all right. Did you call the police?"

"The only thing bothering me is that Luisa would have had to cut the brakes."

"Did she know how?"

"Wait! Amy swears the skinny man in the hoodie, the one from the security tape, was talking to Luisa the night of the murder. Even this morning Amy referred to him as Luisa's boyfriend. Luisa denied it. Made up a story about it being a handyman. And…"

"And what?" said Rebecca.

"A couple staying at the inn said they heard a conversation with the words 'that's why I love you.' What if the skinny man in the hoodie is Luisa's boyfriend. What if he cut the brakes?"

"It's possible."

"And the parrot! When Amy mentioned Dorian, Luisa knew she was referring to a parrot but I'm sure Amy never said Dorian was a parrot. I have to go to the cottage and tell Brianna."

Emily raced out of the cabin and into her Audi. She tried calling the police station but she'd forgotten to charge her phone last night.

Emily ran out to the car and rode to Ruth's cottage. She saw a rental car in the driveway. Brianna was going to have a rental. She ran to the door.

"Emily? I didn't expect to see you so soon. Come in."

"I have to check something. Do you mind if I go into Ruth's bedroom?"

"No. Go ahead. I haven't even been in there myself yet. What do you need?"

"Ruth's copy of the will." She ran into the bedroom and retrieved the will. "Got it."

"What's going on here, Emily?"

"Brianna, Luisa claims she never met you and never worked at the disabled vets' office."

"Of course she knows me."

"And she has the same last name as a man who kidnapped my sister Amy thirty years ago and who recently died in prison. From mental health issues and not getting psychiatric care. He was a veteran. He was her brother."

"Her brother?"

"Yes. Luisa was obsessed with getting the VA hospital built. Ruth put in her will that her estate would cover building it, but then she amended the will after she was scammed by Baltimore. Luisa was irate that she changed the will and had to stop her from filing it."

"Wow. Did you tell the police?"

"Can I use your phone? I'm afraid Luisa might show up when she realizes Ruth could have a copy of the original here in the cottage. Unless she's fled the country by now." She called Megan.

Brianna jumped. "Did you hear that?"

"Hear what?" Emily stood still. "You mean like someone's walking on top of us?"

"What if it's her? What if Luisa got in here before either of us arrived."

"I didn't see another car." Another bang, like a door slamming.

"She has to know we're here. And doesn't seem concerned about keeping herself hidden." Brianna was shaking.

"She'd have to come through here to get to the door. Let's make a run for it. I parked behind you."

They ran out the front door. Emily fumbled with her keys and Brianna slid into the passenger seat. She stepped on the gas and peeled out of the driveway. In the rearview mirror, she saw a car.

Brianna turned and looked over her shoulder. "We're being followed. What are we going to do?"

"It has to be the boyfriend. I know these roads and he's driving a truck compared to my Audi. I've got this." She swerved around a corner.

"He's getting closer."

Emily slammed down on the gas pedal and fought to keep control while staying ahead of the truck. Her hands ached from gripping the steering wheel so tightly.

Brianna screamed. "He's almost caught up to us."

Emily swerved onto a dirt road. The truck did the same. Emily made a sharp U-turn and raced back to the road.

"I'm scared," said Brianna.

"Hold on tight!" Emily floored the Audi. The truck was gaining on them. Another car came at them head on beeping its horn. Emily swerved around it hoping it'd slow down the truck as well.

"I think we lost him," said Brianna. "Wait, no! He's coming at us full speed. He's going to crash right into us!"

Sirens blared. Then they saw a police car racing their way. Another was behind it. Emily pulled off to the side of the road. The second cruiser stopped to make sure they were okay.

"Yes, but there's a truck behind us. Go on. We're okay here."

"Wait right here." The officer took off. Brianna hugged Emily. Soon, it was all over. One of the cruisers raced past them heading into town. The second stopped. Megan and Ron stepped out.

Megan said, "Are you okay?"

"Yes. Did you get them?"

Ron answered. "We got them both. We'll need a statement."

"Anything to get those two locked up for life," said Emily.

Brianna said, "This is the peaceful town my grandmother wanted to retire in? It's not how I remember it as a kid, that's for sure."

Chapter 28

~

Wednesday

The reading of the will went off smoothly. To celebrate, Coralee invited Brianna and the Fox family to the inn for dinner that evening.

Amy ran up and hugged Emily the moment she spotted her. "You came for dinner. To celebrate, right?"

"Not exactly a celebration, but at least Ruth's murderer—or should I say murderers—are behind bars."

"Where's Maddy?"

"She's spending the night over at her friend Jenna's. Let's sit down. I'm hungry."

Brianna and Coralee were at the table. "I made Ruth's favorite dinner as a tribute to her," said Coralee.

Brianna said, "I'm planning a proper funeral and celebration of life. I hope you'll all be there. Meanwhile, this is a nice way to remember my grandmother."

Coralee said, "What are your plans, Brianna? Are you going to sell the cottage?"

"Oh, no. I'm going to live in it and supervise the building of the Ruth Winchester Home for Independent Living. With my psychology and counseling background, who better than me to manage the place."

"That's lovely," said Coralee. "Ruth would be so proud."

"And I'm donating a portion of my inheritance to the Disabled Vets of America. There's enough goodwill, not to mention money, to go around."

Coralee said, "It's such a coincidence how Luisa wound up connecting with Brianna and then the tie-in with your book, Emily. Who'd have imagined."

Emily said, "After Luisa read Emily's book, she came to Sugarbury Falls out of curiosity. She was hoping to talk to Amy and me and learn more about her brother's life while he was out in the woods with Amy. She really loved her brother. Then, she ran into Ruth and Brianna who were here for a long weekend. Luisa and her boyfriend were staying at a motel down the road, but had come to the inn for dinner one night."

"I'm usually good with faces, but I didn't remember them at all," said Coralee.

Emily continued, "She overheard Ruth talking to you about moving here and building something charitable to use as a tax write-off. That's when she got the idea. She followed Brianna back to New York to the disabled vets' office and devised her plan."

"So she wasn't planning on killing Ruth?"

"No," said Emily. "She wanted to sway Ruth into building a veteran's hospital."

"When I offered to introduce her to my grandmother who needed an assistant, she jumped at the opportunity. Seeing the

Veteran's hospital come to fruition was in her mind an homage to her brother, Poppy."

"But Ruth changed her mind," said Coralee.

"Yes, and when she announced it at the book signing, Luisa went ballistic. She called her boyfriend to come help her. He'd been staying down the road. The lawyer had called that night about verifying Ruth's new will. Luisa knew if the new will was filed, the land would be designated for an indie-living facility and not the veteran's hospital. They had to work quickly."

Brianna said, "Luisa's boyfriend is a mechanic. He cut Ruth's brakes and left the note."

Coralee said, "So that's who Amy saw on the second floor."

"And who she heard arguing."

"With whom?"

"With Ruth. Amy was right. Luisa asked Ruth to meet her upstairs to convince her not to change her plans. Ruth wouldn't budge. Her boyfriend tried to talk to Ruth and they wound up arguing."

Coralee said, "What about the note we found in Ruth's cottage? The warning note. From Baltimore?"

"Luisa and her boyfriend planted it to throw us off the trail."

"And I guess I know the rest," said Coralee.

Brianna said, "I'm going to miss Grandma every day. What a senseless murder. I hope the two of them get locked up for life."

"If you need anything, Brianna, we're right down the road. Call on us anytime."

Coralee said, "And I'm not Ruth, but I loved her and she'd want me to be sure you are looked after."

"You've all been wonderful. I'm hungry. Anyone else?"

"Homemade butternut squash soup and grilled cheese on focaccia bread coming right up."

Henry's phone vibrated. "Hello? What? Where are you? I'm coming right over."

Emily said, "Henry, what's wrong?"

"I have to go right now."

"But your dinner…"

"It's an emergency. Get it to-go. I'll meet you back home." He threw his napkin on the seat and stormed out of the dining room.

Coming soon, *The Guilty Course*, Book 7 in the Sugarbury Falls Mystery Series. Here's a preview!

Henry's blood boiled through his veins. He swerved the wheel hard to the left to avoid the tractor trailer heading at him on the narrow mountain road glistening with new rain. That's it. He's a dead man now. His fatherly instincts had never risen to this level of intensity. Or was it insanity?

He swerved to avoid a convertible full of teens, blaring music, and beer. Or so he imagined. Rain and darkness made it impossible to see clearly. He hadn't told anyone, not even Emily, that he had a location on the monster. No need to scare them, or to show his hand. If he moved too soon, the police would say they had no evidence to arrest him—to send the monster back to prison in Chicago. And Detective Ron Wooster, half of the town's detective team, had a personal stake. One wrong move and any potential criminal case would go out the window.

With the rain now falling in sheets, he almost drove right past it. The anemic neon sign barely drew attention to the row of dilapidated rental bungalows. He pulled the Jeep in front, sloshed through the mud, and knocked on Bungalow 13.

"Open up. I know you're in there. You son of a …The police are on the way. If you harm one hair on my daughter's head…" He banged his fist repeatedly against the door. Thunder roared; lightening flashed against the sky.

He took a few steps back, ran at the door. And kicked with all his might. The door gave way. Henry turned on the desk lamp. "Where are you? Where's Maddy?"

About the Author

 Award winning author Diane Weiner is a veteran public school teacher and mother of four grown children. Fond memories of reading mysteries by Nancy Drew and Mary Higgins Clark on snowy weekends in upstate New York inspired her to write books that would bring that kind of joy to others. Being an animal lover, she is a vegetarian and shares her home with two precious cats—Chelsea and Callie. In her free time, she enjoys running, shopping, attending theater productions, and spending time with her family.

Visit **dianeweinerauthor.com** to find out more about the author.